JUL 3 1 2003

Lit

A FIRESIDE BOOK

PUBLISHED BY SIMON & SCHUSTER

New York London Toronto

Sydney Tokyo Singapore

MYSTERY

&

CRIME

The New York Public Library® Book of Answers

Intriguing and Entertaining

Questions and Answers

About the Who's Who

and What's What

of Whodunits

☞

by
JAY PEARSALL

A STONESONG PRESS BOOK

FIRESIDE
Rockefeller Center
1230 Avenue of the Americas
New York, New York 10020

FIRESIDE and colophon are registered trademarks
of Simon & Schuster Inc.
A Stonesong Press Book

Designed by Crowded House Design
Manufactured in the United States of America

ISBN: 1-56865-132-5

For the staff at Murder Ink.,
Meg,
and especially Lauri,
who makes everything flow

Contents

Preface

"Entering the library through its main entrance on Fifth Avenue, we passed between the two big stone lions, and went straight upstairs to the main reading room. Maybe you don't know the layout. There's a grand staircase and lofty corridors, all marble. From the upstairs corridor you go into a vast catalogue room, row on row of little drawers in which are filled the cards on which the books are indexed and cross-indexed. You find the index cards for the books you want and from them you fill out a withdrawal slip, one for each book. Name of book, the author, its index number, your own name, and your address."

The Funniest Killer in Town
by Hampton Stone

Most of us who have even a passing acquaintance with The New York Public Library will recognize the lions, the marble corridors, and Room 315 (card catalog drawers notwithstanding), however unfamiliar the detective fiction of Hampton Stone may be. In fact, *The Funniest Killer in Town* is only one of a number of thrillers that take place in libraries—ranging from personal libraries to large public libraries, including the one on Fifth Avenue. Apparently a mystery with a body in the library has intrigued a variety of writers, just as it did the incomparable Agatha Christie. In the order and dignity of a library, clues can be laid out methodically and violence rips through the quiet fabric. Librarians have been victims and they have turned sleuth—including a Shakespeare-quoting library guard. One of the most original murder weapons is surely a catalog drawer spindle (in "Death Walks in Marble Halls," by Lawrence G. Blochman—a short story using a New York Public Library setting).

This volume, *Mystery and Crime*, joins a number of other books of answers sponsored by The New York Public Library. Its lighthearted, yet all-encompassing approach will appeal to and satisfy the vast numbers of people who enjoy mysteries. According to one librarian at our Mid-Manhattan Branch, that means almost everyone, for by mid-afternoon on any given day some five or six hand trucks of returned detective stories need to be reshelved!

Readers of this book—even those who are hardened addicts of the genre—will find much to intrigue them and new authors and titles that they will want to read. Any public library is a good source for stories of mystery and suspense, new and old. Agatha Christie is still being republished, read, and even assigned in school; readers snatch the latest Sue Grafton or Elmore Leonard off the shelves.

Not only do neighborhood libraries stock, or try to keep the shelves stocked with, mystery stories, but so do The Research Libraries of The New York Public Library. These extensive noncirculating collections provide scholars with a comprehensive picture of how the genre has developed and changed. Much of the writing, according to several librarians, is on par with the best fiction being published today, and the setting—whether ancient Rome or a modern archaeological dig—is usually very carefully researched. Then, too, librarians at The Research Libraries always have in mind future generations of scholars. Nothing will give readers of the twenty-first century a better slant on the 1980s and 1990s than to see what people were *really* reading.

This book can be read and enjoyed again and again. The reader will get new ideas of novels and authors to explore. It is ideal for sharing—for swapping tidbits of information (Hercule Poirot's height; how many women Travis McGee has slept with; who first proclaimed that "crime does not pay"). Whether we are talking of novels of crime and suspense, of police stories, spy fiction, or thrillers—this book touches on them all—the genre captivates a large segment of the population; librarians, we are told, prominent among them.

Introduction

Why a book of answers about mysteries?

To answer that question we should try to figure out why people read mysteries in the first place. It has been said that people enjoy mysteries because they get to live vicariously through the detective and experience both the thrill of adventure and the satisfaction of arriving at the correct solution. Others say that mysteries offer them a chance to learn something interesting while they read. Still others say they enjoy the puzzle aspect of mystery.

Rex Stout, who created one of world's greatest detectives in Nero Wolfe, had a theory that people who didn't like mysteries were anarchists. I think what Stout meant by this is that people who don't like mysteries don't appreciate order. For where else but in a mystery can you find such perfect order? Unlike so much of modern literature—or life for that matter—mysteries have a very definite plot, and by the conclusion, loose ends have been tied up, a logical solution reached, justice served, and order restored.

Every day dozens of people walk into Murder Ink.—the store of which I'm lucky enough to be the proprietor—and about half of them have questions, mostly along the lines of, "What is the name of that one-armed detective who owns a bar in Cincinnati?" And that question is almost always followed by, "Who wrote that?" and, "Has he or she written a new one?" After years of looking things up or listening to the bookstore owner's greatest resource—other knowledgeable customers just waiting to show off—you learn a thing or two and eventually you have a brain full of interesting (you hope) and useful (you pray) information.

Although there have been many great questions asked at Murder Ink., this book isn't merely a compilation of them, but is instead a gathering together of what is interesting, clever, astounding, and hilarious in the mystery genre. It's the kind of information that you have to share with someone, that you want to read out loud, or shout across the room, "Hey, did you know that Agatha Christie had trouble getting her first mystery published?"

For our purposes I have included all types of what mystery author and critic Julian Symons has called "sensational literature," that is, books that deal with violent ends in a sensational way, whether they be called detective stories, police stories, spy stories, thrillers, or suspense novels. There are certainly distinctions to be made, but it seems both safe and fair to group Sherlock Holmes, Sam Spade, and Modesty Blaise in the same general category.

The chapters themselves are pretty specific, with the early ones being more or less chronological. It didn't seem right only to include works that are still in print, since there seems to be little reason involved in publisher's decisions about what they keep and what gets tossed. If you are intrigued by something you find in these pages, don't be discouraged if the book is out of print. Your local library or favorite used bookstore may be able to help you find exactly what you're looking for or recommend something else you might find interesting. All you have to do is ask.

Jay Pearsall

Sherlock Holmes and Forerunners

Who was the first detective in crime fiction?
Edgar Allan Poe's character Chevalier C. Auguste Dupin is generally given that honor. Making his first appearance in the story "The Murders in the Rue Morgue" (1841), Dupin was poor but of "illustrious parentage" and would sometimes remain in his room for a month at a time, stewing over a puzzle. Dupin appears only twice more, in the stories "The Mystery of Marie Roget" (1842) and "The Purloined Letter" (1845). After Poe opened the door, writers Wilkie Collins, Eugène Sue, and Arthur Conan Doyle followed with detective fictions of their own.

But what about Wilkie Collins? I've always heard that his *Moonstone* was the first mystery. What gives?
Poe wrote "The Murders in the Rue Morgue" in 1841 and Collins wrote *The Moonstone* in 1868. The confusion came about when none other than T. S. Eliot wrote that Collins was the first, longest, and best writer of detective fiction.

Where did Poe's "The Murders in the Rue Morgue" first appear in print?
On April 1, 1841, in the Philadelphia periodical *Graham's Magazine*.

What early detective was a Russian exile?
The creation of M. P. Shiel, Prince Zaleski is a noble Russian exile and one of the most learned and brilliant detectives ever. He employs a devoted Ethiopian servant, Ham, and lives in a bizarre, palacelike home where he is lulled by the "low, liquid, tinkling of an invisible music box," while in "the semi-darkness a very faint greenish lustre radiated from an open censer-like 'lampas' of fretted gold in the centre of the domed encased roof." That's easy for him to say. See *Prince Zaleski* (1895).

Can you name the first thief to serve as a main character in detective fiction?
Most would say E. W. Hornung's Raffles, but actually Colonel Clay beat out Raffles by about two years. Clay was a master of disguise and could become anything from a Scottish parson to a Mexican seer. See *African Millionaire* (1897), by Grant Allen.

What was the first American magazine devoted entirely to detective fiction?
That honor goes to *The Old Captain Collier Library,* first published on April 8, 1883.

How did Arthur Conan Doyle come to create the character of Sherlock Holmes?
Doyle was a rather unsuccessful doctor when in 1886 he made some notes about a pair of characters named Sherrinford Holmes and Ormond Sacker, who were later to become Sherlock Holmes and Dr. Watson. These notes finally became "A Study in Scarlet," which was rejected by several publishers before it was accepted by Ward, Lock, & Co. and published in *Beeton's Christmas Annual* of

1887. Here is how the acceptance letter read:

Dear Sir,

We have read your story and are pleased with it. We could not publish it this year as the market is flooded at present with cheap fiction, but if you do not object to its being held over till next year, we will give you twenty-five pounds for the copyright.

Yours faithfully,
WARD, LOCK, & CO.
Oct. 30th. 1886

Doyle later recalled, "It was not a very tempting offer, and even I, poor as I was, hesitated to accept it." But hoping this story would open the door for him he did accept the offer and was never paid more than that original twenty-five pounds.

Was Sherlock Holmes based on a real person?
Dr. Joseph Bell, a surgeon at the Edinburgh Infirmary, was the model for Holmes in terms of appearance, manner, and style. Primarily, though, Holmes was very much like Doyle—who solved several real-life murder cases. Doyle also borrowed from other fictional characters: Holmes's use of disguises comes from François Eugène Vidocq (*Memoirs of Vidocq, French Police Agent,* 1828), his style of interpreting thoughts from Edgar Allan Poe (*Tales,* 1845), and his deductive ability from Emile Gaboriau (*Monsieur Lecoq,* 1880).

Sherlock Holmes always seems to have the answer. Does he know everything?
No, not at all. When Watson makes a list of Holmes's strengths and weaknesses he writes "nil" for the great detective's knowledge of literature, philosophy, and astronomy. Watson does note, however, Holmes's "profound" knowledge of chemistry as well as his skills in botany, geology, and anatomy.

Didn't Arthur Conan Doyle kill off Sherlock Holmes only to revive him at a later date?

Yes. Holmes dies in "The Final Problem" (1893) and makes his return in *The Hound of the Baskervilles* (1902). The original Sherlock Holmes stories were serialized in *The Strand* magazine, and when the issue appeared containing the shocking news of Holmes's death, groups of young men wearing black armbands marched on the magazine's offices and "Let's Keep Holmes Alive" clubs sprang up in various American cities.

At the time Doyle wrote to a friend saying, "I have such an overdose of him that I feel towards him as I do towards pâté de foie gras, of which I once ate too much, so that the name of it gives me a sickly feeling to this day." Pressure from fans as well as offers of enormous sums of money lured Doyle to bring Holmes back.

Did Sherlock Holmes have a favorite book?

In "The Sign of the Four" (1889) he says, "Let me recommend a book—one of the most remarkable ever penned. It is Winwood Reade's *Martydome of Man.*"

What was the name of Sherlock Holmes's landlady?

Her name is Mrs. Martha Hudson, and she called Sherlock Holmes "the worst tenant in London."

Where did Holmes live?

221B Baker Street.

When was Sherlock Holmes born?

Holmes was born January 6, 1854, in Mycroft, North Riding, Yorkshire.

What is the name of the poor man who rejected the first Sherlock Holmes story?

He is the long-forgotten mystery author James Payn. At the time

(1886) he was editor of *Cornhill Magazine.*

What did Sherlock Holmes think of women?
In "The Sign of the Four" (1889) he says, "Women are never to be entirely trusted—not the best of them."

Where did Holmes say to Watson, "Data! Data! Data! I can't make bricks without clay"?
He said it, rather impatiently, in the story "The Adventure of the Copper Beeches" (1882).

In which contemporary pastiche is the detective the illegitimate child of Sherlock Holmes and Irene Adler?
Son of Holmes (1986), by John T. Lescroart. Not only is the detective, one Auguste Lupa, the son of Holmes and Adler, but it is implied that he is the young Nero Wolfe. Get it? Auguste Lupa . . . Nero Wolfe.

What did Sherlock Holmes look like?
Doyle describes him as being very tall—over six feet—but so thin that he seemed considerably taller. He had a "thin razor-like face," with "a great hawk's-bill of a nose," and two small eyes, set close together.

When a friend of Sir Arthur Conan Doyle's became fatally ill while in the midst of writing a story, Doyle was asked to finish it. Can you name that story?
"Hilda Wade," which was started by Doyle's friend Grant Allen in 1899 and finished by Doyle that same year.

In what mystery were clues written on a young woman's back?
Rider Haggard's "Mr. Meeson's Will" (1904).

Who was Craig Kennedy, "the American Sherlock Holmes"?
The creation of Arthur B. Reeve, Kennedy was a professor at Columbia University. Reeve predicted many advances in criminology, and Kennedy was certainly one of the first "scientific" detectives. It has been said that Kennedy's extreme popularity might also have something to do with the fact that a young girl named Elaine appeared in many of the stories and always had to be rescued from the trickiest of situations. Kennedy makes his first book appearance in *The Gold of the Gods* (1915).

Who was the turn-of-the-century lawyer often described as part Abraham Lincoln, part Robin Hood, and part Uncle Sam?
Arthur Train's character Ephraim Tutt, who appeared in more than a dozen volumes of short stories between 1920 and 1945, and who said of the legal profession, "The law offers greater opportunities to be at one and the same time a Christian and a horse-trader than any other profession."

When Harry Houdini and Arthur Conan Doyle met and performed a séance, what was the outcome?
Houdini didn't really believe in séances, but Lady Doyle convinced him that they should try to contact his mother. Lady Doyle acted as the medium and took down the message. The Doyles thought the event was a success, but Houdini knew otherwise—the message was in English; his mother knew only Yiddish.

The Golden Age

What was the "Golden Age"?
The Golden Age of detective fiction occurred between the two world wars, when several crucial developments changed the genre forever. The stories became more literate and the detectives more believable—no longer were they persons of superhuman intellect who could look at someone's shoes and determine where they had just been by the type of dirt collected there. Also, much more emphasis was put on period and character as opposed to merely constructing a clever puzzle. Two influential authors of the Golden Age are an Englishman, E. C. Bentley (*Trent's Last Case,* 1913) and an American, S. S. Van Dine (*The Benson Murder Case,* 1926). Other huge authors of the age include: Agatha Christie, Edgar Wallace, Dorothy L. Sayers, Freeman Wills Croft, H. C. Bailey, and Leslie Charteris.

Why was Jacques Futrelle's character, Professor Augustus S. F. X. Van Dusen, called the "Thinking Machine"?
Van Dusen appears in two collections of stories, *The Thinking Machine* (1907) and *The Thinking Machine on the Case* (1908), and is

an example of the detective as omniscient superman—to the point of absurdity. In the first story in which he appears, he denigrates the game of chess by saying he could "take a few hours of competent instruction and defeat a man who has devoted his life to it." A game is arranged with the world champion, Tschaikowsky, who after the fifth move stops smiling and after the fourteenth says, "You are not a man; you are a brain—a machine—a thinking machine." From then on Professor Van Dusen is called the "Thinking Machine."

Has any publisher or author ever offered a reward for coming up with a solution to a mystery?
Part of Edgar Wallace's advertising promotion for his book *The Four Just Men* (1905) was a reward of £500 to anyone who could come up with the solution to it. This offer was great for sales but ultimately resulted in a financial disaster that drove Wallace into bankruptcy. One should note that in the 1920s and 1930s Wallace was known as the "King of Thrillers" and supposedly one out of every four people in England reading a book was reading a Wallace.

In what mystery story was Malvino the Magician engaged to perform for the "fifty little millionaires" at the Pegasus Club?
That would be "Blind Man's Buff" in *The Adventures of the Infallible Godahl* (1914), by Frederick Irving Anderson, one of the great writers of American mystery short stories. Malvino, born to eternal darkness—he was said to have no eyes—was tall and slender and always wore a black silk mask over his face. Godahl (who was sort of an American Raffles) was the only man who truly recognized Malvino's greatness.

Who was the "Canary" in S. S. Van Dine's *The Canary Murder Case* (1927)?
The Canary was a noted blond Broadway entertainer who was found strangled to death in her apartment. The suspects included four of her admirers.

Where did S. S. Van Dine's character Philo Vance live?
He lived in the top two floors of a mansion on East 38th Street in Manhattan.

What did the poet Ogden Nash use to rhyme with Vance?
Nash wrote, "Philo Vance/Needs a kick in the pance."

When did Arsène Lupin fall in love for the first and only time?
In *The Memoirs of Arsène Lupin* (1925), Lupin, under the name of Ralph d'Andrezy, falls in love with the exquisitely beautiful Josephine Balsamo, Countess of Cagliostro.

Which detective's tools of the trade included such items as jars of water, garlic, and bebe ribbons?
William Hope Hodgson created the character Carnacki, who was a psychic detective and a ghost finder. He appeared in a couple of stories and a book called, of course, *Carnacki, the Ghost Finder* (1913).

Who was the "Correspondence-School Detective"?
Ellis Parker Butler's Philo Gubb had a diploma from the Rising Sun Detective Agency's Correspondence School. Gubb's specialty was the disguise that fooled no one, as well as absolute butchery of the English language. See *Philo Gubb, Correspondence-School Detective* (1918).

Who was "the Dream Detective"?
Sax Rohmer created Moris Klaw, who would lie down and sleep at the scene of the criminal act in order to absorb the circumstances of the original crime. Klaw was often suspected of being a fraud, yet he never failed to nail the guilty party. See *The Dream Detective* (1920).

Who was "the Old Man in the Corner"?
The nameless Old Man in the Corner was a true armchair detec-

tive. He solved mysteries from a London tea shop, never visiting a crime scene but merely listening to a young reporter, Polly Burton, who narrated the mysteries. See *Old Man in the Corner* (1902), by Baroness Emmuska Orczy.

What early detective, both a doctor and a lawyer, had as his constant companion his research kit, which was referred to as "the invaluable green case"?

Dr. John Thorndyke, the creation of R. Austin Freeman. He was handsome, tall, and athletic, with excellent eyesight and acute hearing. He was an expert in all things that would be useful to a detective including anatomy, botany, archaeology, ophthalmology, and Egyptology—and he was also quiet and kind. The invaluable green case contained chemicals and tiny instruments. See *Dr. Thorndyke's Case-Book* (1923).

In what whodunit was a cask found at the London docks containing gold coins and a woman's hand?

Freeman Wills Crofts's *The Cask* (1920). Crofts was one of the best plot constructors ever to lift a pen, but the easiest way to spot his murderers is to look for the character with the most airtight alibi. *The Cask* is a masterpiece in terms of logical detection and attention to detail.

In what mystery did the murderer, a surgeon, kill his victim by inserting a tiny glass bulb filled with poisonous gas (which will burst at some later time) into his heart?

This and many other improbable things happened in *The Broken O* (1933), by Carolyn Wells. Her books are filled with hidden doors, sliding panels, and secret passageways. The really scary thing is that she once wrote a manual called *The Technique of the Mystery Story* (1913).

What author was brave enough not only to let his detective fall in love with the prime suspect but also to come up with a com-

pletely wrong ingenious solution to the crime?
E. C. Bentley was the author and Philip Trent was the fallible detective who starred in *Trent's Last Case* (1913).

What mystery did the novelist Christopher Morley call "one of the finest studies of murder ever written"?
Frances Iles's *Before the Fact* (1932), which Morley went on to call "a masterpiece of cruelty and wit." What makes it stand out is its concern with motivation and characterization more than strictly plot and its inverted nature, since you know from the very start who did it.

What is the "had-I-but-known" school of mystery novel?

The master of this school was Mary Roberts Rinehart (see, for example, *The Circular Staircase*, 1908). In this type of mystery there is usually a detective, but he is often less important than the plucky young woman who hears strange noises in the night and overhears sinister conversations. She often finds herself trapped in the house with the murderer—"I knew he was creeping up on me, inch by inch"—and she almost always survives to stumble upon some clue that solves the mystery.

What is the "cozy," or "tea cozy"?

The cozy is a branch of the amateur school in which the violence is limited and usually "offstage." There is generally only one body, all the characters are urbane and civilized, the crime scene is often an English country house, and tea is almost certainly taken. Agatha Christie's Miss Marple books are perfect examples of the cozy.

What is a "police procedural"?

In the most liberal sense a police procedural features a real police officer or detective as opposed to an amateur or private detective. In a stricter sense the police procedural is the type of book that has been perfected by Ed McBain and Joseph Wambaugh. In these mysteries the hero is a police officer who utilizes scientific techniques; personality is often downplayed, with the star of these books being modern forensics. In the police procedural there are no outlandish explanations of events—instead, fingerprints and blood samples are taken, witnesses questioned, and confessions obtained.

Which author wrote the most "locked room" mysteries?

John Dickson Carr was the master of the locked-room school, where the murder is perpetrated in an apparently sealed room. This type of murder story is always more concerned with the technique rather than the actual murder, and common themes include the murderer convincing the victim to kill himself or herself, gas leaking under the door, and the employment of various hidden mechanical devices. Occasionally there is no murder at all, only lethal coincidences.

What does the term "inverted mystery" mean?

In the inverted mystery we see a crime committed at the beginning of the story and instead of waiting until the end to unmask the perpetrator, the author reveals him immediately. There is no mystery, really, and not much surprise, but the interest of watching the detective at work is enhanced by our prior knowledge, and the fun comes from watching the detective discover and follow clues that lead to the criminal. This type of mystery was invented by R. Austin Freeman in *The Singing Bone* (1912). A fine modern example is *The Suspect* (1985), by L. R. Wright. For an interesting twist on this theme try *A Dark Adapted Eye* (1986), by Barbara Vine, a pseudonym of Ruth Rendell.

Sometimes it seems that authors don't play fair; you think you've figured out who did it, and then they pull a fast one.

Aren't there any rules for writing mysteries?

There's nothing official, mind you, but mystery author and editor Father Ronald A. Knox, in his *Detective Story Decalogue* (1928), established the best-known set of rules for writing detective fiction. Father Knox's Ten Commandments are as follows:

I. The criminal must be someone mentioned in the early part of the story, but must not be anyone whose thoughts the reader has been allowed to follow.

II. All supernatural or preternatural agencies are ruled out as a matter of course.

III. No more than one secret room or passage is allowable. I would add that a secret passage should not be brought in at all unless the action takes place in the kind of house where such devices might be expected.

IV. No hitherto undiscovered poisons may be used, nor any appliance which will need a long scientific explanation at the end.

V. No Chinese must figure in the story. (Editor's Note: This rule was not intended to be racist but was simply a response to one of the most hackneyed conventions of cheap detective stories of the day.)

VI. No accident must ever help the detective, nor must he ever have an unaccountable intuition which proves to be right.

VII. The detective must not himself commit the crime.

VIII. The detective must not light on any clues which are not instantly produced for the inspection of the reader.

IX. The stupid friend of the detective, the Watson, must not conceal any thoughts that pass through his mind; his intelligence must be slightly, but very slightly, below that of the average reader.

X. Twin brothers, and doubles generally, must not appear unless we have been duly prepared for them.

The Amateur Detective

Can you explain the term "amateur detective?"
The most famous of all amateur detectives is Arthur Conan Doyle's
Sherlock Holmes, who was modeled after Poe's detective C. Auguste Dupin. The amateur detective is usually independently
wealthy, eccentric, and of superior intellect. He is not a private investigator, nor does he work for any police organization—he, or
she, rarely works at all—and he usually has a "Watson," or helper,
who narrates the story and tells us how brilliantly our mastermind
sleuth is going about solving the case. Rex Stout's Nero Wolfe, S. S.
Van Dine's Philo Vance, and Agatha Christie's Hercule Poirot and
Miss Marple are all examples.

**What British amateur detective claimed that he could solve a
murder even before the crime had been committed?**
Dagobert Brown, the creation of Delano L. Ames. Brown made this
claim in *She Shall Have Murder* (1948), the first in a series of twelve
books. He never really supported his boast.

What mystery series features an amateur detective and his two Siamese cats, Koko and Yum Yum?
The Cat Who . . . series, by Lilian Jackson Braun, in which Jim Qwilleran ("Qwill") is the detective. The cats are likable and smart, but not supernatural; the catlike things they do are interpreted by Qwill as clues and Qwill is always quick to give the cats credit for solving the crime.

What amateur detective is an oral surgeon?
Rick Boyer's detective, Dr. Charles Adams, has a lucrative practice in the upscale community of Concord, Massachusetts. Boyer won an Edgar Award for *Billingsgate Shoal* (1982).

· **Which holdover from the Golden Age consistently wrote with a pessimistic view of married life?**
Harry Carmichael would often uncover a veil of marital bliss to expose jealousy, greed, and infidelity. His best books feature an insurance assessor, John Piper, and a crime reporter, Quinn. A good one to start with is *Candles for the Dead* (1973).

What detective series features Sir Abercrombie Lewker, who is a famous actor-manager and Shakespearean scholar?
Glyn Carr created Lewker, nicknamed "Filthy"—get it?—who besides being a thespian is also a passionate mountain climber. The victims in Carr's books are often done in on a steep rock face.

In which Ellery Queen mystery do a nudist camp, a Balkan blood feud, and a demented Egyptologist figure as elements?
The Egyptian Cross Mystery (1932), one of the most bloody and bizarre of the Queen books.

Which three detectives did Ellery Queen consider to be the greatest of all time?
Doyle's Sherlock Holmes, Poe's C. Auguste Dupin, and G. K.

Chesterton's Father Brown.

Which amateur detective works as the resident manager of the Beaumont, New York City's top luxury hotel?
Hugh Pentecost's character Pierre Chambrun, who must often solve murders in order to save the fictitious hotel's reputation. Chambrun made his debut in *The Cannibal Who Overate* (1962).

Which amateur detective is most likely to be heard using the epithet "Oh my Aunt!"?
Most likely it would be H. C. Bailey's Reggie Fortune, who is a physician and an adviser to Scotland Yard on medical matters.

Isn't there a series that features Dr. Samuel Johnson and James Boswell?
Yes. Lillian de la Torre wrote twenty-nine stories featuring realistic and historically accurate portraits of Johnson and Boswell. The first book of stories is *Dr. Sam: Johnson, Detector* (1948).

Who was the "Codfish Sherlock"?
Phoebe Atwood Taylor's Asey Mayo, a retired seaman. His job as factotum for one of Cape Cod's wealthiest tycoons allowed him time to untangle the nets of many a fishy crime. See *The Cape Cod Mystery* (1931).

Which amateur detective has a job as a meter reader for a northern California power company?
Vejay Haskell, a creation of Susan Dunlap, works for Pacific Gas & Electric reading meters. This job—and her curious nature—allows her to witness many strange things, sometimes murderously strange. She first appeared in *The Bohemian Connection* (1985).

Who is Hal Johnson, the Library Fuzz?

He is the creation of James Holding, who was a prolific short-story writer. His detective, Hal Johnson, bumps into murder while tracking down overdue library books. "The Book Clue" (1984) is one of the interesting Hal Johnson stories.

What fictional amateur detective's death received front-page news coverage from *The New York Times*?

On Wednesday, August 6, 1975, the front page of *The New York Times* reported the death of Hercule Poirot, who was, of course, Agatha Christie's detective. The first lines of the story read, "Hercule Poirot, a Belgian detective who became internationally famous, has died in England. His age was unknown."

How many Perry Mason novels did Erle Stanley Gardner write?

Eighty-two. The first was *The Case of the Velvet Claws* (1933) and the last was *The Case of the Postponed Murder* (published posthumously in 1973). He also wrote twenty-nine novels under the pseudonym A. A. Fair; nine books about a small-town D. A., Doug Shelby; and a dozen or so others with characters Terry Clane, Sheriff Bill Eldon, and Gramps Wiggin.

What is the name of Perry Mason's secretary?

Della Street.

What was the name of William Faulkner's detective?

Faulkner's detective was attorney Uncle Gavin Stevens, who appears in two novels, *Intruder in the Dust* (1949) and *Knight's Gambit* (1949). He was a Phi Beta Kappa graduate of Harvard who returned to Yoknapatawpha county, and he was also an excellent chess player.

Why was Nick Charles, of Dashiell Hammett's Nick and Nora, called "the thin man"?

He wasn't. Someone in Hollywood decided that "the thin man" was catchy and used it in all the titles of those Nick (William Powell) and Nora (Myrna Loy) movies. There was even a TV show called *The Thin Man*, even though the thin man was just a missing corpse in the original novel and movie.

Agatha

Did Agatha Christie ever receive any rejection slips?
Yes. Shortly after World War I an unpublished writer named Agatha Christie sent a manuscript entitled *The Mysterious Affair at Styles* to a London publisher. It was rejected, and Christie sent it out five more times before John Lane at the Bodley Head accepted it and the world was introduced to Hercule Poirot. The book was a modest success, and as others followed Christie gradually became a leader in the mystery genre. By the end of World War II, Agatha Christie was a household name.

In *Peril at End House* (1932), how many attempts are made on Nick Buckley's life?
Four. A heavy portrait falls from her wall; a boulder crashes past her into the sea; the brakes fail on her car; and a direct assassination attempt is made.

What was the evidence of the silk hose in *Cards on the Table* (1936)?

Poirot concluded that Anne Meredith was capable of theft when he presented her with nineteen pair of hose and after her inspection of them only seventeen pair remained.

Which of Agatha Christie's many books did she dedicate to readers who wondered what had happened to Tommy and Tuppence Beresford?
By the Pricking of My Thumbs (1968). The pair of fictitious characters had appeared in two earlier Christie books, *N or M?* (1941) and *The Secret Adversary* (1922), and apparently many readers had missed them.

What theory did Poirot come up with about the sequence of the deaths of Sir Bartholomew Strange and Stephen Babbington in *Murder in Three Acts* (1934)?
Poirot found it very suspicious that Strange, a doctor, died *after* Babbington, not before. Assuming that Babbington was poisoned, Poirot reasoned that the poison must have been intended for Strange.

When did Agatha Christie die?
On January 12, 1976. Just prior to her own death she managed to kill off one of her two main detectives, Hercule Poirot, in *Curtain* (1975). It was Christie's wish that he not be resurrected after her death.

In *The Mystery of the Blue Train* (1928), what is Poirot's theory on the nobleman as a suspect for Ruth Kettering's murder?
Poirot reasons that the nobleman *attempted* to steal Ruth's jewels, but that he did not have the drive to be a robber or a murderer.

How tall is Agatha Christie's detective, Hercule Poirot?
He is a small man, only five feet four inches tall.

What is the name of Hercule Poirot's lodgings?
In *Evil Under the Sun* (1941) it is Whitehaven Mansions, but in other books it is referred to as Whitehorse Mansions.

What does Jane Marple's usual attire consist of?
She is often seen wearing a black brocatelle with lace on the front of the bodice.

How does Hercule Poirot like his toast prepared?
In neat little squares.

Parker Pyne used to advertise in the newspaper. What was the message of his ads?
After retiring as a government statistician, Pyne wished to employ his talents to good use. He placed an ad in the Personals column which read: "Are You Happy? If Not Consult Parker Pyne. . . ." Pyne first appeared in 1934 in the story "The Case of the Middle-Aged Wife."

Which mythical Greek figure is alluded to in *Nemesis* (1971)?
Clytemnestra.

What English poet is referred to in *The Mirror Crack'd* (1962)?
Alfred Lord Tennyson, and the poem alluded to is "The Lady of Shallot."

What is the name of the luxury yacht in *The Regatta Mystery* (1939)?
The Merrimaid.

At the beginning of *There is a Tide . . .* (1948) Mrs. Cloade learns of Hercule Poirot's existence by two means. Can you

name them?
She saw his photograph in *The Picture Post* and his initials appeared
repeatedly on her Ouija board.

**Can you name all of the Agatha Christie movies made for the
big screen (no television productions allowed)?**

Die Abenteuer G. m. b. H.	1928
The Passing of Mr. Quinn	1928
Alibi	1931
Black Coffee	1931
Lord Edgeware Dies	1934
Love from a Stranger	1937
And Then There Were None	1945
Love From a Stranger	1947
Witness for the Prosecution	1957
The Spider's Web	1960
Murder, She Said	1962
Murder at the Gallup	1963
Murder Most Foul	1964
Murder Ahoy	1964
Ten Little Indians	1965
The Alphabet Murders	1966
Endless Night	1972
Murder on the Orient Express	1974
Ten Little Indians	1975
Death on the Nile	1978
Agatha	1979
The Mirror Crack'd	1980
Evil Under the Sun	1982
Ordeal by Innocence	1984
Appointment with Death	1988
Ten Little Indians	1989

Private Eyes, Grifters, and Dames

What, exactly, is a hard-boiled detective?
A hard-boiled detective is a private investigator (read PI, private eye, dick, gumshoe, etc.), an alienated loner, a man who lives by a code and carries a piece. He is tough-talking and good with his fists. Dashiell Hammett's Sam Spade, Raymond Chandler's Philip Marlowe, and Mickey Spillane's Mike Hammer are classic examples, and their direct descendants include John D. MacDonald's Travis McGee, Ross Macdonald's Lew Archer, and Robert B. Parker's Spenser. The best of today's class of the hard-boiled school include authors James Lee Burke, James Crumley, and James Ellroy.

Are there any female hard-boiled detectives?
There are some excellent ones. Try the works of Marcia Muller, Sue Grafton, and Sara Paretsky.

Who was the first hard-boiled detective?
Carroll John Daly's character Race Williams is generally considered to be the first hard-boiled dick. Race became famous for aphorisms

such as, "You can't make hamburger without grinding up a little meat." Race Williams first appeared in *Black Mask* magazine in 1922.

What hard-boiled detective is apt to hear his friends call out, "Hi, Noon!"
That would be Michael Avallone's character Ed Noon, who appears in thirty novels, all of them packed with lousy jokes, puns, movie and baseball references, and mind-numbing and questionable grammar like the following: "She had tremendous hips and breasts encased in a silly short black fur jacket and calf-high boots." Avallone is also the creator of *The Man from U.N.C.L.E.* and *Mannix,* as well as the author of *Keith Partridge, Master Spy* (1971), *Women in Prison* (1961), and *Never Love a Call Girl* (1962).

Are there any private eyes who are kind and gentle?
Just a few. One of the kindest is Timothy Dane, a character created in 1951 by William Ard. Dane is a different kind of gumshoe: young, naive, tender with women, bad in a fight, and often in need of help to get out of a jam. The best of the Dane books is *Hell Is a City* (1955).

What's the most unusual review you've ever seen for a hard-boiled mystery?
In 1939 the critic John Mair reviewed *No Orchids for Miss Blandish,* by James Hadley Chase, as follows:

Guys Rubbed Out	22 (with a rod, 9; with a tommy-gun, 6; with a knife, 3; with a blackjack, 2; by kicking, 1; by suicide, 1)
Guys Slugged Bad	16 (in the face or head, 15; in the guts, 1)
Guys Given a Workover	5 (with blunt instruments, 3; with a knife, 1; with burning cigarettes, 1)
Dames Laid	5 (willing, 3; paid, 1; raped, 1)

What is the real name of Dashiell Hammett's character the Continental Op?

Hammett never names his fat, middle-aged detective, who is featured in several short stories and one of the best mystery novels ever written, *Red Harvest* (1929).

What did Sam Spade look like?

Not like Humphrey Bogart, who played Spade in the 1941 version of *The Maltese Falcon*. Dashiell Hammett describes Spade on the first page (1930) as looking "rather pleasantly like a blond satan." His jaw is long and bony, his chin a jutting V under the more flexible V of his mouth. His nostrils curve back to make another smaller V. His yellow-green eyes are nearly horizontal. He is six feet tall but the severely rounded slope of his shoulders make his body seem as broad as it is thick.

Side note: Hammett received about $7,000 for the film rights to *The Maltese Falcon,* which was made three times: once in 1931 starring Bebe Daniels and Ricardo Cortez, then in 1936 as the retitled *Satan Met a Lady,* and finally in 1941, directed by John Huston, starring Humphrey Bogart and Mary Astor.

Who is Sam Spade's partner in *The Maltese Falcon* (1930)?

Well, for a few pages it's Miles Archer. A beautiful redhead walks in. Spade takes the case. Next thing you know, Archer is dead.

What best-selling private investigator is most likely to take time off from gumshoeing to make an omelet?

Robert Parker's Spenser, besides having the requisite virtues of persistence and toughness, is also an excellent cook. He's also rather literate—in *The Widening Gyre* (1983) alone he cites Arnold, Tennyson, Hopkins, Eliot, Frost, Stevens, and Kris Kristofferson. Did we mention that Spenser is also a former professional boxer and a sensitive modern man?

Who is the other detective that Rex Stout writes about? You know, the one who isn't Nero Wolfe?

Tecumseh Fox, a Westchester County private detective who works out of large farm where he keeps so many animals that his neighbors call it "the Zoo." Fox appears in three of Stout's books, *Double for Death* (1939), *Bad for Business* (1940), and *The Broken Vase* (1941).

It seems that John D. MacDonald's character Travis McGee is always falling into bed. Could you tell us just how many women he sleeps with?
In the twenty-one Travis McGee books there is reference to (or strong evidence of) ol' dawg Travis sleeping with around fifty-three women—plus "a few ladies."

Could you be more specific? How about names?
Really? Okay, here goes—a complete Travis McGee sexual history, as revealed by the novels of John D. MacDonald: Travis's first sexual experience was at age sixteen with a "loud chubby" girl named Lolly. Since then he has slept with Susan, Missy, Teresa, Lois Atkinson, Molly Bea Archer, Cathy Kerr, Joanie, Nina Gibson, Isobel Webb, Mary "Skeeter" Keith, Dana Holtzer, Niki, "Junebug" Proctor, Betty O'Donnell Borlika, Nora Gardinao, Felicia Novaro, Constance Melgar, Vidge, Merrimay Lane, Heidi Geis Trumbill, Gloria "Glory" Doyle, "Puss" Killian, Helena Pearson, Penelope Woertz, Mary Catherine, Janice Holton, Mary Lo Ching, Maria Amparo Celestina Rodriguez De La Vega, Lady Rebecca Diven-Harrison, Elena Del Vega, Betsy Kapp, Mary Dillon, Jillian Brent-Archer, Teddie, Jeannie Dolan, Mary Alice McDermit, Cathy Kerr, Linda Lewellen Brindle, Marian Lewandowski, R. N., Cindy Birdsong, Billy Jean Bailey, Sister Stella, Gretel Tuckerman Howard, and Lady Vivian Stanley-Tucker, as well as an heiress in Las Vegas; Sir Thomas's wife, a stewardess, a school teacher, two tourist ladies, an Avon lady, and a hostess at Beef 'n It.

Just to make things clear, Travis never slept with prostitutes and didn't believe in group sex. He also says at some point that relationships should "rest solidly on trust, affection, respect," though he has "faltered from time to time." You should also know that he does not consider women as "pneumatic, hydraulic, terrace toys."

Just one more. What is the name of Travis McGee's houseboat?
The Busted Flush.

In which Raymond Chandler novel does Philip Marlowe become involved in the murder of a millionairess who has had six husbands?
The Long Goodbye (1954). This was Chandler's next to last book, and before Marlowe solves the murder he is engulfed by enormous wealth, corruption, and cruelty.

What detective of the 1940s was a two-fisted, woman-chasing, hard-boiled private eye who never drank anything stronger than milk?
Nowadays there are several, but back in the 1940s only one came to mind, and it would have to be Humphrey Campbell of *Build My Gallows High* (1946), by Geoffrey Homes.

What mystery series features a professional burglar who is also a bibliophile?
Lawrence Block's Bernie Rhodenbarr is the burglar who likes books. One of the best books in the series is *The Burglar Who Liked to Quote Kipling* (1979).

What is the name of the fat man in *The Maltese Falcon*?
Kasper Guttman, who is described as follows: "The fat man was flabbily fat with bulbous pink cheeks and lips and chins and neck, with a great soft egg of a belly that was all his torso, and pendant cones for arms and legs." Sydney Greenstreet played him in the 1939 movie version.

Who is described as "the toughest, hardest, strongest, fastest, sharpest, biggest, wisest, meanest man west of the Mississippi River"?
Dashiell Hammett's Continental Op, who has also been described

as "fat and forty." Depends on the light, I guess.

What female private detective of the 1940s weighs more than 200 pounds, is in her sixties, and swears like a longshoreman?
That would be Bertha Cool. A creation of A. A. Fair, a pseudonym of Erle Stanley Gardner, Bertha Cool appeared in twenty-nine novels (*The Bigger They Come,* 1939; *Bats Fly at Dusk,* 1942; *Give 'em the Ax,* 1944; etc., etc., etc.) with her partner, Donald Lam.

What heavy-set private detective smokes vile black cigars and wears a gold toothpick that hangs from a chain around his rather significant neck?
That would be "the terror of crooks from coast to coast," Jim Hanvey. See *Jim Hanvey, Detective* (1923), by Octavus Roy Cohen.

To what is Fredric Brown referring to when he writes about "the fabulous clipjoint?"
Chicago. One of Brown's characters, Am (Ambrose) Hunter, a detective and poker player, refers to the windy city as a fabulous clipjoint. See *Mrs. Murphy's Underpants* (1963) and *The Fabulous Clipjoint* (1947).

Who is the Chicago-based detective known only as "Mac"?
Mac was a Chicago cop until he solved a crime the mob didn't want solved and he was fired. He became a private detective and worked out of an office near Chicago's North Side. See *Sad Song Singing* (1963), by Thomas Dewey.

Who is "the Human Encyclopedia"?
Oliver Quade, who fends off the bill collectors by selling a one-volume *Compendium of Human Knowledge.* Quade has a great mind for trivia and a truly impressive ability for running into murder. Quade appears in *Brass Knuckles* (1966), by Frank Gruber.

What was the first gangster novel?
Little Caesar (1929), by W. R. Burnett, chronicles the rise and fall of Cesare Rico Bandello from his beginnings as "just a lonely yegg, sticking up chainstores and filling stations," to his brief glory as the leader of a Chicago gang.

Wasn't there a mystery about a hit man who was hired to rub out a fifteen-year-old nymph who was blackmailing the mob?
So Young, So Wicked (1957), by Jonathan Craig. Craig was what you'd call a journeyman, having written over one hundred stories and fourteen novels.

Who is the San Diego private investigator who seldom carries a gun because of his bad temper?
Wade Miller's Max Thursday hardly ever carries a gun because of his tendency to lose control and shoot first and, you know, ask questions later. *Guilty Bystander* (1947) is the first Max Thursday book.

Isn't there a private detective who is half Norwegian and half Japanese?
Yes, Trygve Yamamura, who was born in Hawaii and works out of a small office in Berkeley, California. See *Perish by the Sword* (1959), by Poul Anderson.

What is the name of the dame in *The Maltese Falcon*?
The beautiful young woman introduces herself as Miss Wonderly, but it turns out that her real name is Brigid O'Shaughnessy.

I've been reading Richard Stark's series featuring the professional thief Parker. Can you tell me his first name?
He doesn't have one—but Richard Stark's real name is Donald E. Westlake. Try *The Man with the Getaway Face* (1963).

In what mystery does a character count a lot of money, including a bunch of twenty-five-dollar bills?
In *The Violent World of Mike Shayne* (1965), by Brett Halliday, the following lines appear: "He poured himself a drink and counted the money. It came to ten thousand even, mostly in fifties and twenty-fives."

I know that John D. MacDonald's Travis McGee is described as "spectacularly huge," but just how big is he?
He is six feet four and a bit, weighs between 205 and 212 pounds, and his suit size is 46 Extra Long, with a 44-inch inseam and 34-inch waist: His shirt collar is 17 1/2 inches and his sleeve 36 inches.

What is the name of the black detective who is from Detroit and works out of a storefront operation in San Francisco?
Carver Bascombe, who often does his detective work in and around the San Francisco art world, has so far appeared in eight books by Kenn Davis. The first in the series is *The Dark Side* (1976).

Who was "Hollywood's hottest hawkshaw"?
Dan Turner, a hard-boiled dick created by Robert Leslie Bellem. Turner appeared in dozens of stories written for the pulps.

What is the meaning of the title of James M. Cain's *The Postman Always Rings Twice* (1934)?
Well, there is no postman in the book—the title has to do with the quirky nature of chance. H. R. F. Keating said the title was "Cain's sideways acknowledgment of the power of fate, of chickens coming home to roost."

Why are the early mystery magazines like *Black Mask* and *Dime Detective* called "pulps"?

These magazines were popular in the 1920s and 1930s, playing to a literate but not literary market. They were printed on cheap, grainy wood-pulp paper, hence the name, "pulps." Raymond Chandler and Dashiell Hammett both got their starts writing for these magazines.

What pulp author created the characters Otis Beagle, Simon Lash, and Johnny Fletcher?

Frank Gruber—but how could you forget Oliver "the Human Encyclopedia" Quade?

What are some other names private eyes are called besides hard-boiled detectives?

Gumshoe, private dick, sleuth, hawkshaw, sherlock, shamus.

What do we know about the private life of Raymond Chandler's detective Philip Marlowe?

Not much. Only that he has no family or friends and that he changes his address every couple of years and enjoys playing chess. We know he went to college for a while and used to work for the district attorney. Chandler's emphasis is much more on action and plot than on the characters' past.

Who was the first woman to write an American detective novel?
Metta Victoria Fuller Victor, who wrote *The Dead Letter* (1867) under the name Seeley Regester.

But what about Anna Katherine Green? I've always heard that she was first.
Anna Katherine Green didn't write *The Leavenworth Case* until 1878, some eleven years after Metta Victor. Green's father was a lawyer and she was consequently quite familiar with legal and criminal matters. Her detective, Grace, is somewhat lively, but the story is remarkably dreary and sentimental.

What famous striptease artist wrote mysteries?
Rose Louise Hovick, writing under her stage name, Gypsy Rose Lee, concocted two mysteries: *The G-String Murders* (1941) and the less successful *Mother Finds a Body* (1942). We say "concocted" because it is widely believed that Lee's former press agent, Craig Rice, actually wrote these books.

In which mystery is the body found in a bathtub, naked except for gold pince-nez?
Dorothy L. Sayers's Lord Peter Wimsey is on his way to a rare book auction in *Whose Body* (1923) when he is called to the scene by an architect who discovered the body.

In what mystery does a bedridden inspector investigate the 400-year-old murder, allegedly by Richard III, of the Princes in the Tower?
Josephine Tey's *The Daughter of Time* (1951). Critic Anthony Boucher called it "one of the permanent classics in the detective field."

In Sarah Caudwell's books her narrator, Professor Hilary Tamar, is never referred to in terms of gender. Is Hilary a man or a woman?
Most readers have a theory about this one way or the other, but since Ms. Caudwell won't tell, we're afraid we can't help you. The books in the series are *Thus Was Adonis Murdered* (1981), *The Shortest Way to Hades* (1984), and *The Sirens Sang of Murder* (1989).

Who was Agatha Christie's favorite American mystery writer?
Elizabeth Daly, who borrowed many elements of the British cozy of the Golden Age and transported them to New York of the 1940s. Her detective, Henry Gamadge, is an author and a bibliophile, who makes his debut in *Unexpected Night* (1940).

Does Sue Grafton, the author of "A" Is for Alibi, "B" Is for Burglar, etc. really expect to get through the entire alphabet?
She does indeed, although it will probably take her into the next millennium (until around 2009). So far she's completed *"K" Is for Killer,* and besides the two you already mentioned, she's done *"C" Is for Corpse, "D" Is for Deadbeat, "E" Is for Evidence, "F" Is for Fugitive, "G" Is for Gumshoe, "H" Is for Homicide, "I" Is for Innocent,* and *"J" Is for Judgment.* At her current pace of one book a year, she'll finish

the year before her seventieth birthday. Ms. Grafton's character Kinsey Millhone doesn't seem to be aging in real time, but even if she were, she'd end the series well before she turned sixty. "X," Ms. Grafton has hinted, will be for "xenophobe." By the way, as the result of an extremely small print run, a first edition of *"A" Is for Alibi* in excellent condition would run you about $1,000.

What mystery author stopped writing a series because her detective's depression became too disturbing?
Linda Barnes says of her character Michael Spraggue, "Because I had chosen to make Spraggue an amateur, I had the continuing problem of involving him legitimately in his cases. I solved this by killing off many of his friends and relatives. His subsequent depression became difficult to deal with and I sought a new hero." Spraggue appears in four books, the first of which is *Blood Will Have Blood* (1982).

What is the name of the female protagonist in Daphne du Maurier's *Rebecca* (1938)?
She is a second wife, living under the shadow of the mysterious and brilliant—and dead—Rebecca. She is never named.

When was Dorothy L. Sayers born?
Dorothy L. Sayers, the creator of Lord Peter Wimsey, was born July 13, 1893, in Oxford, England. She was a precocious child, learning Latin at the age of seven, and one of the first women to graduate from Oxford. She was a copywriter at an advertising agency before she started writing mysteries.

In which of Sayers's books does Harriet Vane meet Lord Peter Wimsey?
They meet in *Strong Poison* (1930), work together in *Have His Carcase* (1932), announce their engagement in *Gaudy Night* (1935), and are married in *Busman's Honeymoon* (1937).

What is the motto on Lord Peter Wimsey's coat of arms?
It reads, "As my whimsy takes me."

Who is often referred to as "America's Agatha Christie"?
Mignon G. Eberhart, though we suspect that this accolade was first bestowed by an optimistic copywriter. Her books, starting with *The Patient in Room 18* (1929), are really much more of the Mary Roberts Rinehart school of had-I-but-known suspense novels, than the cozy tradition of Christie.

Which of her mysteries did Agatha Christie write just after slipping on an icy train platform and falling onto the tracks?
Murder on the Orient Express (1934). According to her second husband's memoirs, Christie fell in Calais and was actually *under* the Orient Express. Luckily, the train wasn't moving and the porter was able to fish her out before the train started again.

What is the U.S. title of Ngaio Marsh's *Surfeit of Lampreys* (1940)?
Death of a Peer (1941). "Lamprey" refers to a family in the book and we can only guess that it sounded strange to an American editor's ear. "Surfeit" was probably deemed too difficult a word for the American public.

How does one correctly pronounce "Ngaio," as in Ngaio Marsh?
Pronounce it "Ni-yo," as in "hi-yo."

Which author of a female private eye series has written teleplays, including an episode of *Rhoda*?
Sue Grafton wrote an episode of *Rhoda* entitled "With Friends Like These" (1975). She also wrote several episodes for the series *Seven Brides for Seven Brothers* (1982–83). Grafton has said that her experience in writing for television is the reason she will never sell her

books or the use of her character, Kinsey Millhone, to Hollywood. She knows better.

Which star of the London stage also wrote mysteries?
Dulcie Gray, who can list among her leading roles the part of Miss Marple. Besides having a distinguished stage career she wrote several mysteries, the first of which was *Murder on the Stairs* (1957).

Which American author writes a very successful series set in England? Hint: All of her titles are the names of real British pubs.
Taken from English country inns and pubs, such as *The Man with a Load of Mischief* (1981) and *I Am the Only Running Footman* (1987), Martha Grimes's titles have become her trademark. Her detective is Superintendent Richard Jury of Scotland Yard.

If I were going to read only one HIBK, (that is, a "had I but known" novel), what should that be?
In the HIBK the damsel fails to tell the police what she knows and so finds herself facing fresh perils. One of the better ones is Mabel Seely's witty novel *The Listening House* (1938).

What mystery series features a single woman who is an English professor at a large urban university?
Amanda Cross (a pseudonym of Carolyn Heilbrun, a retired Columbia University English professor) writes a series featuring Kate Fansler, whose investigations take place in or around the university or literary world. Later in the series, Fansler marries a lawyer named Reed Amhearst. Kate Fansler first appears in *In the Last Analysis* (1964).

What is the name of the female San Francisco–based private investigator who is part Shoshone Indian?

Marcia Muller's Sharon McCone, who is notable for being one of the earliest and longest-lasting female hard-boiled private investigators. McCone made her debut in *Edwin of the Iron Shoes* (1977).

What can be found in the purse of Elizabeth Peters's amateur sleuth, Jacqueline Kirby?

Kirby is a middle-aged librarian at a large eastern university. Her purse is repeatedly described as containing her cigarettes, aspirin, knitting, a paperback mystery, smelling salts, and a police whistle. Try *The Seventh Sinner* (1972).

Besides Jacqueline Kirby, Elizabeth Peters has another detective, Vicky Bliss, who has several lovers including one who is an art thief and swindler. What's his name?

Sir John Smythe. At the end of *Trojan Gold* (1987) he leaves our Ms. Bliss a ring and disappears.

What female private investigator opened her agency with money inherited from her aunt?

Valerie Frankel's detective, Wanda Mallory, opened Do It Right Detective Agency with money inherited from her aunt. Wanda lives in Brooklyn, New York, with a cat and a pearl-handled .22-caliber pistol named "Mama."

What detective runs a mystery bookstore in Broward's Rock?

Caroline G. Hart's detective, Annie Laurance, runs Death on Demand, a mystery bookstore in an island community off the South Carolina coast.

What female sleuth is a chief medical examiner?

Patricia D. Cornwell's detective Dr. Kay Scarpetta is the Chief Medical Examiner of Virginia. Scarpetta makes her debut in *Postmortem* (1990).

What amateur investigator is an assistant professor of English at Vassar?
Susan Kenney's detective, Roz Howard, who first appears in *Garden of Malice* (1983).

What female author's mysteries tend to have Scottish themes even though they are set in Virginia?
Sharyn McCrumb's. Her character Elizabeth MacPherson starts out as a graduate student in the first book (*Sick of Shadows,* 1984) and later gets a Ph.D. in forensic pathology.

What female crime novelist once wrote: "Creative people do not pass moral judgements—at least not at once—on what meets their eye. There is time for that later in what they create, if they are so inclined, but art has nothing to do with morality, convention or moralizing"?
Patricia Highsmith in *Plotting and Writing Suspense Fiction* (1966). She has also written such masterpieces of suspense as *Strangers on a Train* (1950), *The Talented Mr. Ripley* (1955), and *Found in the Street* (1986).

Who created the first modern British female private investigator?
That honor goes to P. D. James. Her private eye Cordelia Gray first appears in *An Unsuitable Job for a Woman* (1972).

Rogues and Scoundrels

What famous rogue is described as a "condor-eyed, electric-witted and amazingly successful prowler among the perilous labyrinths of the shady side of life"?
Smiler Bunn "makes his living off society in a manner always devious and sometimes dark, but never mean." Generally, he steals from the rich and gives to himself and his partner, Henry Black. See *The Smiler Bunn Brigade* (1916), by Bertram Atkey.

What safecracker believes that as long as he refrains from using his skills in Paris, that city will always be a refuge?
This superstitious safecracker's name is Bourke, who was created by Louis Joseph Vance. Bourke is quite a ladies' man, and he hates his red hair because it so easily identifies him. See *The Lone Wolf* (1915).

Who is the Man of Forty Faces?
Hamilton Cleek—really the Prince of Mauravania—can change his appearance by contorting his face and is one of the most brazen

and talented criminals ever to face Scotland Yard. At one point he asks not to be called "The Vanishing Cracksman," instead preferring "The Man Who Calls Himself Hamilton Cleek." When the newspapers comply, he sends them information stating when his next robbery will take place and promising to give a small bit of the loot to Scotland Yard the next morning. He does this successfully every time until he falls in love and abandons crime. See *The Man of Forty Faces* (1919), by Thomas W. Hanshew.

Who was Raffles?

Raffles was the greatest rogue in all of crime literature. He was called "the Amateur Cracksman" and was a British gentleman, comfortable both with aristocracy and a supposedly unopenable safe. Raffles stole for fun, excitement, intellectual stimulation, and of course for the money, though he often gave it away to a friend in need. Late in his career he gave up crime, worked on the side of the law, and ultimately met his end in the Boer War. The first of the Raffles books was *The Amateur Cracksman* (1899), by E. W. Hornung.

Who was the American counterpart of Raffles?

The Infallible Godahl was America's consummate criminal. He was never caught, nor ever even suspected, and thus only he knew what a master of crime he truly was. When he was not "working" he was a New York socialite. See *The Infallible Godahl* (1914), by Frederick Irving Anderson.

Can you name the female counterpart of Raffles?

Fidelity Dove led a very successful and loyal band of male thieves, and Detective-Inspector Fason called her "the coolest crook in London and then some." See *The Exploits of Fidelity Dove* (1935), by Roy Vickers. There was also a Henriette Van Raffles of *Mrs. Raffles* (1905), by John Kendrick, which was a burlesque of the E. W. Hornung *Amateur Cracksman* novels.

Can you name another female thief, more of a Robin Hood type?
Edgar Wallace's character Four Square Jane stole only from the very rich and gave all the spoils to charity. Because she was a master of disguise, no one knew what she looked like, though Superintendent Dawes of Scotland Yard called her the cleverest criminal he had ever gone up against. See *Four Square Jane* (1928).

What villain lives by these two precepts: "Never volunteer" and "Bullshit baffles brains?"
Eric Ambler's Arthur Abdel Simpson, who appears in *The Light of Day* (1962) and *Dirty Story* (1967). These rules to live by are the only things he inherited from his father. Simpson also says, "I have only really been arrested ten or twelve times in my whole life."

Who was Flambeau?
Flambeau is a character who appeared in some G. K. Chesterton short stories. He was a huge Frenchman, "a figure as statuesque and international as the Kaiser," whose best crimes were robberies and whose most humorous moments came when he utilized his great strength—such as when he ran down the street carrying a policeman under each arm. See "The Blue Cross" (1911).

What French villain was called "the Lord of Terror" and described as "a modern Mephistopheles"?
Fantomas, who first appeared in France in 1910, was the creation of journalists Marcel Allain and Pierre Souvestre. Fantomas was an evil genius who used science and technology to gain wealth and power. The last story about him was published in 1963.

What was the name of the villainous mastermind in Wilkie Collins's *The Woman in White* (1860)?
Count Fosco, who was extremely fat and kept pet mice, which scampered about on his waistcoat. But beneath this comic appearance was a determined and sinister man.

Who was "the gentleman-cambrioleur?" Hint: Jean Paul Sartre called him "the Cyrano of the underworld."
Arsène Lupin, created in 1907 by Maurice Leblanc, was a marvelous combination of strength, courage, and dastardly intelligence. *Cambrioleur,* for those of you who aren't up on your French, means "burglar." Lupin first appears in *Arsène Lupin: Gentleman-Cambrioleur* (1905).

What did Carl Peterson, the opponent of Bulldog Drummond, look like?
Well, Peterson was—you guessed it—a master of disguise, so we don't really know. At the conclusion of *The Final Count* (1926) he met his end, and we read: "For full five seconds did he stand there before the end came. And in that five seconds the mask slipped from his face, and he stood revealed for what he was. And of that revelation no man can write." Sorry. The author is "Sapper," whose real name was Herman Cyril McNeile.

What rogue had the longest run in crime fiction?
In 1937 John Creasey, writing as Anthony Morton, created the man-about-town jewel thief, John Mannering, aka "the Baron." The Baron first appears in *Meet the Baron* and forty-nine books later says goodbye to crime in *Love for the Baron* (1979).

Who was "the Napoleon of Crime"?
None other than Conan Doyle's Professor James Moriarty, who was the archenemy of Sherlock Holmes. Moriarty was "a man of good birth and excellent education, endowed by nature with a phenomenal mathematical faculty." But, alas, "a criminal strain ran in his blood."

I know there have been many con men, but have there ever been any confidence women?
A few. One of the most charming is Miss Lucilla Edith Cavell Teatime, a creation of Colin Watson. Miss Teatime has that perfect

combination of respectability and a love of the scam. "People instinctively approved of her, for there was in her appearance the flattering suggestion that she had taken pains to spare one personally the spectacle of yet another dumpy, disgruntled, defeated old woman." See *The Flaxborough Crab* (1969).

What rogue believed that danger is good for you?
Leslie Charteris's character the Saint. He believed that danger makes you feel more intensely alive.

What was the Saint's real name?
Simon Templar. He started out as a rogue but, as so often happens, he later became good and worked on the side of the law. The Saint first appeared in *Meet the Tiger* (1928).

What master thief steals only things of no value?
Nick Velvet demands $20,000 for a job—$30,000 if it's especially dangerous. His heists have netted such objects as a sea serpent, the water from a swimming pool, and an entire baseball team. His wife, Gloria, believes he works for the government. The author of the Nick Velvet stories (there are dozens of them) is Ed Hoch. See *The Thefts of Nick Velvet* (1978).

Who was the first female crook in crime fiction?
Madame Koluchy was the first, making her debut in *The Brotherhood of the Seven Kings* (1899) by L. T. Meade and Robert Eustace.

What is the name of the good-hearted thief who tries to steal the Balabomo diamond?
That's John Dortmunder, a creation of Donald E. Westlake, who attempts to steal the Balabomo diamond in *The Hot Rock* (1970). Dortmunder always gets involved in intricately absurd burglary

plots that are foiled by bad luck, inept henchmen, or his own good heart, which won't ever allow him to cause real harm.

Who was Fu Manchu?
Fu Manchu, also known as the Devil Doctor, was believed to be a descendent of the Manchu dynasty. He was a diabolical fiend whose goal was to become the emperor of the world. See *The Mystery of Dr. Fu-Manchu,* by Sax Rohmer (1913).

Who was the female Fu Manchu?
Sumuru, who first appears in *Sins of Sumuru* (1950), also by Sax Rohmer.

Candlesticks and Curare

What are some of the more unusual poisons used in mysteries?
Douglass Clark was the hands-down champ of esoteric poisons and has used such toxins as castor-oil beans (*Premeditated Murder*, 1975), peppercorns (*Golden Rain*, 1980), salad oil (*The Gimmel Flask*, 1977), and plain old water (*Sick to Death*, 1971, and *Dread and Water*, 1976). Runner-up would be V. C. Clinton-Baddeley, who, in *Death's Bright Dart* (1967), concocted a poison brew of ants.

Which mystery features oxalic acid in the sugar?
Christopher Bush's *The Tea Tray Murders* (1934).

What is the most unusual murder weapon used in a mystery?
Perhaps a frozen leg of lamb. In Roald Dahl's "Lamb to the Slaughter" a woman kills her husband by striking him with a frozen leg of lamb—and then cooks it and serves it to investigators who worked late and missed their dinner hour.

Which Agatha Christie mystery features a dart dipped in prussic acid?
Death in the Air (1935).

And what poison is put into the marmalade in Christie's *A Pocket Full of Rye* (1953)?
Taxine goes in the marmalade, and for good measure cyanide is put into the sugar.

In which mystery is the murder weapon a strain of deadly Italian bees?
Gerald Heald's *A Taste of Honey*. The bees are used by an apiarist to kill a man who has already used the same type of bees to commit his own undetectable murder.

What mystery features a group of characters who discuss determinism and free will while trying to find a bottle of olive oil that has been poisoned before someone cooks dinner with it?
Charlotte Armstrong's 1957 Edgar Award–winning *A Dram of Poison*. The poison comes out of a locked laboratory cabinet and is identified only as "No. 333."

In which mystery does an insane murderer known as "the Cat" strangle his victims with cords of Indian silk?
The Cat of Many Tales (1949) finds Ellery Queen pitted against one of his most dangerous foes.

Which Fu Manchu novel employed weapons ranging from crude missiles to occult animal magnetism?
The rather racist Fu Manchu series consisted of fourteen books. The one in question is *The Hand of Fu Manchu* (1917).

In which Perry Mason novel are two separate murder victims

found, each clutching a bloodshot glass eye?
That would be *The Case of the Counterfeit Eye* (1935). The prime suspect, Peter Brunold, himself having only one real eye, owns a bloodshot glass eye for the "morning after." Perry Mason takes the case, but finds himself in almost as much trouble as his client—his fingerprints are found on one of the murder weapons.

What is the cleverest method of disposing of a body in crime fiction?
There are many good ones, but our favorite appears in Jack Finney's *Time and Again* (1970). Some folks may cry, "Foul play!" because of the element of science fiction in the book, but we like it anyway. The hero is able to travel through time and go back far enough to prevent his enemy's parents from ever meeting, thus getting rid of the body by uncreating it. It's tough to beat that.

In which of Ngiao Marsh's mysteries did the killer use "a colorless liquid" to kill the victim?
Final Curtain (1947). The colorless liquid was thallium acetate.

Didn't another of Marsh's books feature poison that was put into a perfume atomizer?
Yes, and the name of the book is *False Scent* (1959). The poison used was hexa-ethyl-tetra-phosphate.

What, exactly, is curare?
Commonly called moonseed, curare's scientific name is *Strychnos toxifera,* and it comes from any number of South American trees of the genera *Chondodendron* and *Strychnos*. It is used medicinally as a muscle relaxant and by some South American Indians as an arrow poison. Curare is not harmful if swallowed but kills instantly if it enters the bloodstream. There is no antidote.

In what thriller does the author arm his assassin with bullets specially loaded with a blob of mercury?
Frederick Forsyth did this in *The Day of the Jackal* (1971). These bullets were supposed to pack quite a wallop, but according to a gun expert they wouldn't work.

On the Beat

In what mystery classic does the investigating police detective fall in love with the murder victim after the victim is already deceased?
Detective Mark McPherson falls in love with the title character in Vera Caspary's *Laura* (1943). This masterful and delightful book is especially interesting for two reasons: the fascinating character of Laura and the multiple points of view from which the story is told.

What mystery series takes place in Harlem and features two black detectives named Coffin Ed Johnson and Grave Digger Jones?
Coffin Ed Johnson and Grave Digger Jones were created by Chester Himes. These two tough and violent New York City detectives appear in nine books, starting with *For the Love of Isabelle* (1957) and ending with *Plan B* (1983).

Who is the most incompetent of all police detectives?
That would probably have to be Joyce Porter's Inspector Wilfred

Dover, who is more interested in food and drink than he is in solving crimes. In *Dover One* (1964), Porter notes, "The fact that his career as a detective had endured, and even flourished in a mild way, was almost entirely due to the fact that most criminals, incredible as it may seem, were even more inept and stupid."

Who is an independently wealthy detective who works for the Los Angeles Police Department?
Dell Shannon's Lieutenant Luis Mendoza inherited a fortune from his grandfather and joined the force out of an inner rage for bringing order to a chaotic society. See *The Ace of Spades* (1961).

What Scotland Yard Inspector is known as "Handsome"?
Roger "Handsome" West, with his blue eyes, broad shoulders, and eternally youthful appearance, is one good-looking guy. The incredibly prolific John Creasey drops "Handsome" into some forty-odd books, including *Holiday for Inspector West* (1946).

What mystery series features the overweight, hard-drinking police chief of Rocksburg, Pennsylvania?
The Mario Balzic series written by K. C. Constantine. Most police procedurals take place in urban settings, but Constantine has created an excellent series set in a small town in which he focuses more on the characters' thoughts and emotions than on the usual "detective" work and laboratory results. Try *The Man Who Liked Slow Tomatoes* (1982).

What British author shares with his character a love of crossword puzzles, Wagner, and A. E. Housman?
Colin Dexter, the creator of Inspector Morse. Dexter writes clever and complicated plots and fills his books with considerable humor. Morse's motto is: "Everything fits, you see, once you turn the pattern upside down." Try *The Silent World of Nicholas Quinn* (1977).

How does Joseph Wambaugh know so much about cops?
Before Wambaugh hit it big as an author, he was a police officer in Los Angeles.

What British policeman would prefer tossing back a pint of lager or playing a round of darts to solving crimes?
Probably most, but the one who comes to mind is Leo Bruce's detective Sergeant William Beef. Try *Case for Three Detectives* (1936).

Murder by Quotation

What hard-boiled mystery novel opens with this line: "When I finally caught up with Abraham Trahearne, he was drinking beer with an alcoholic bulldog named Fireball Roberts in a ramshackle joint just outside of Sonoma, California, drinking the heart right out of a fine spring afternoon"?
The Last Good Kiss (1978), by James Crumley.

What female private eye once said, "I don't take small cases. I have a decadent lifestyle"?
Susan Dunlap's character Kiernan O'Shaughnessy, in *Pious Deception* (1989). She is a forensic pathologist who runs her own detective agency in La Jolla, California.

Who first said, "Crime does not pay"?
Dick Tracy. Chester Gould was the author credited with coining the phrase.

What private investigator said, "Once a chump, always a chump"?
Sam Spade, in *The Maltese Falcon* (1930), by Dashiell Hammett.

Where would you find this quotation: "You might think it wasn't real nice to kick a dying man, and maybe it wasn't. But I'd been wanting to kick him for a long time, and it just never had seemed safe till now."
Jim Thompson's *Pop. 1280* (1964), a dark novel about Potts County sheriff Nick Corey, who starts out as what appears to be a mildly corrupt lawman. Later we discover he is both deeper and darker.

What author is credited with coining the phrase, "You can't win them all"?
Raymond Chandler, whose character Roger Wade quips to Edward Loring in *The Long Goodbye* (1953). According to *The Concise Oxford Dictionary of Proverbs* (1982), Chandler was the first to put the phrase into print. It did not come into common use until the 1960s.

What mystery opens with this line, "I was in the Tupinamba having a bizocho and coffee when this girl came in"?
James M. Cain's *Serenade* (1937).

Who said, "Never start an argument with your hands in your pockets"?
Harold Adams's character Carl Wilcox, in *The Naked Liar* (1985).

What author wrote, "If one cannot command attention by one's admirable qualities at least one can be a nuisance"?
Margery Allingham, in *Death of a Ghost* (1934).

Who wrote, "One nude woman is beautiful but a nudist colony is only silly"?
Donald E. Westlake wrote it. Fred Filtch says it. *God Save the Mark* (1967) is the book.

Which Ross Thomas character said, "If you're in trouble, you're alone"?
Stan Burmser says it to Michael Padillo in *Cast a Yellow Shadow* (1967).

What British sleuth said, "Antiques, women and survival are my only interests. It sounds simple, but you just try putting them in the right order"?
Jonathan Gash's antiques dealer–detective, Lovejoy, in *The Grail Tree* (1979).

Who said, "Everything ends"?
Philip Nore, in Dick Francis's *Reflex* (1980).

What hard-boiled mystery opens with this line: "It was about eleven o'clock in the morning, mid October, with the sun not shining and a look of hard wet rain in the clearness of the foothills"?
The Big Sleep (1939), by Raymond Chandler.

What hard-boiled private eye said: "You sat and you listened or you stood and you listened. And when the calluses got thick enough so you didn't fidget, then you could be a private detective"?
Paul Pine, in *Halo in Brass* (1949), by Howard Browne.

What sleuth said, "Facts are piffle"?
Dr. Gideon Fell, in *The Crooked Hinge,* by John Dickson Carr (1938).

What Belgian detective gets credit for the lines, "It is completely unimportant. That is why it is so interesting"?
Hercule Poirot says this to Dr. Sheppard in *The Murder of Roger Ackroyd* (1926), by Agatha Christie.

Who said, "That's the point of quotations, you know: one can use another's words to be insulting"?
Professor Kate Fansler, in *The Theban Mysteries* (1971), by Amanda Cross.

What espionage classic opens with this line: "A Frenchman named Chamfort, who should have known better, once said that chance was a nickname for Providence"?
Eric Ambler's *A Coffin for Dimitrios* (1939).

What famous British sleuth said, "Mediocrity knows nothing higher than itself; but talent instantly recognizes genius"?
None other than Sherlock Holmes, in *The Valley of Fear* (1914), by Arthur Conan Doyle.

Who said, "It is better to be the head of a live sardine than the tail of a dead trout"?
Don Belisario, in *The Big Fish* (1938), by Francis Beeding.

What novel of suspense opens with this line: "The train tore along with an angry, irregular rhythm"?
Strangers on a Train (1950), by Patricia Highsmith.

What mystery includes this line: "He felt like yesterday's newspaper left out in the rain"?
Swamp Sister (1961), by Robert Edmond Alter.

In what thriller does the counterintelligence chief say to his operative: "What we were, never was. What we did, never happened"?
These words are spoken to Matt Helm in *Death of a Citizen* (1960), by Donald Hamilton.

What private eye uttered this gem: "Nothing wrong with Southern California that a rise in the ocean wouldn't cure"?
Lew Archer in *The Drowning Pool* (1950), by Ross Macdonald.

Didn't Lew Archer also have something funny to say about not sleeping with people who have more problems than you do?
Actually, it is advice given to Lew Archer and the exact quote is: "Never sleep with anyone whose troubles are worse than your own." The book is *Black Money* (1966), by Ross Macdonald. By the way, Macdonald borrowed the line from Nelson Algren.

What suspense thriller opens with this famous line: "Last night I dreamt I went to Manderley again"?
Rebecca (1938), by Daphne du Maurier.

Who said, "I don't mind a reasonable amount of trouble"?
Sam Spade, in *The Maltese Falcon* (1930), by Dashiell Hammett.

Who said, "All detective work is sneaking. That's why only gentlemen and cads can do it"?
Keith Innes, in *The Rising of the Moon* (1945), by Gladys Mitchell.

Who tells detective Amos Walker, "The road to hell is smooth as glass"?
John Alderdyce, in *Angel Eyes* (1981), by Loren D. Estelman.

What female private eye says, "Rule number something or other—never tell anybody anything unless you're going to get something better in return"?
V. I. Warshawski, in *Deadlock* (1984), by Sara Paretsky.

What ultra-hard-boiled crime novel opens with the line, "The first time I killed someone, I was scared"?
Shella (1993), by Andrew Vachss.

Who said, "What use is an honest lawyer when what you need is a dishonest one"?
Professor Krom, in *Send No More Roses* (1977), by Eric Ambler.

In which Ruth Rendell book does a character say, "Some say life is the thing, but I prefer reading"?
Giles Mont says it in *A Judgement in Stone* (1977).

What very proper sleuth says, "It is a gentleman's first duty to remember in the morning who it was he took to bed with him"?
Lord Peter Wimsey, in *Busman's Honeymoon* (1937), by Dorothy L. Sayers.

In which Nero Wolfe book does Wolfe keep saying, "Any spoke will lead an ant to the hub"?
In *Fer-de-Lance* (1934), by Rex Stout.

What suspense novel opens with the line, "I returned from the city about three o'clock that May afternoon pretty well disgusted with life"?
The Thirty-Nine Steps (1915), by John Buchan.

Who said, "You see, but you do not observe"?
Sherlock Holmes, in "A Scandal in Bohemia" (1892), by Arthur Conan Doyle.

Who said, "Life has consequences"?
"Milo" Milodragovitch, in *Dancing Bear* (1983), by James Crumley.

Who wrote, "Extravagance is a two-dollar cigar. Waste is to light it with a dollar bill"?
Michael Butterworth, in *The Man Who Broke the Bank at Monte Carlo* (1983).

Which Agatha Christie mystery opens with this line: "Mrs. Ferrars died on the night of the 16th—17th September—a Thursday"?
The Murder of Roger Ackroyd (1926).

Which Christie novel uses as its chapter headings lines from the nursery rhyme that begins, "One, two, buckle my shoe"?
In the U. S. it was called *The Patriotic Murders* (1941), but it's the original U.K. title that makes this question easy: *One, Two, Buckle My Shoe* (1940).

Who wrote the line: "A bullet can give a man a terrific case of indigestion, frequently ending in a trip to the boneyard"?
Robert Leslie Bellem, in the story "Diamonds of Death" (1950).

Who said, "The fool in a hurry drinks his tea with a fork"?
Charlie Chan, of course, in *Keeper of the Keys* (1932).

Who said, "I think perhaps all of us go a little crazy at times"?
Norman Bates, in *Psycho* (1959), by Robert Bloch.

What agent of British Intelligence said, "Beauty draws me with a single hair if it is blonde enough"?
Tommy Hambledon, in *They Tell No Tales* (1941), by Manning Coles.

Who said, "In the heart of every man there lurks the germ of a crook"?
Race Williams, in *The Tag Murders* (1930).

Can you name the source of the following dialogue:
    "Virgil is a pretty fancy name for a black boy like you. What do they call you around home where you come from?"
    "They call me Mr. Tibbs."
Chief Gillespie and Virgil Tibbs in *In the Heat of the Night* (1965), by John Ball.

Who wrote this gem: "The next day dawned bright and clear on my empty stomach"?
Michael Avallone wrote it. Ed Noon said it. The source is *Meanwhile Back at the Morgue* (1960).

In what thriller does this line appear: "Every man at the bottom of his heart believes that he is a born detective"?
The Power-House (1916), by John Buchan.

Which mystery of the had-I-but-known school opens with this

line: "This is the story of how a middle-aged spinster lost her mind"?
The Circular Staircase (1908), by Mary Roberts Rinehart. This book is often dismissed by those who haven't read it. It is worth reading.

Who wrote the line: "If Botesdale was on the premises, he might have raised objections to the murder of his wife"?
Miles Burton (a pseudonym for John Rhode) wrote it in *A Will in the Way* (1947).

What mystery begins with this declaration: "I am going to kill a man. . . ."?
The Beast Must Die (1938), by Nicholas Blake. It turns out that the man the narrator wants to kill is the hit-and-run driver who killed his son.

What mystery contains this bungled bit of description: ". . . saw the sunken eyes between the Judge's oddly flattened nose"?
H. R. F. Keating's *Inspector Ghote Draws a Line* (1979). We've all had that kind of day, haven't we?

In which James Bond novel does the following appear: "Bond's knees, the Achilles' heel of all skiers, were beginning to ache"?
On Her Majesty's Secret Service (1963), by Ian Fleming.

Who wrote the line: "Charlotte Street runs north from Oxford Street, and who can blame it"?
Len Deighton wrote it in *Horse Under Water* (1963).

What mystery includes the following disclaimer: "This is a work of fiction. All names and characters are either invented or used fictitiously. The events described are purely imaginary,

although the accounts of topless creamed-corn wrestling are based on fact"?
This appears in Carl Hiaasen's *Strip Tease* (1993).

What detective can be credited with this line: "Nobody called, nobody came in, nothing happened. Nobody cared if I died or went to El Paso"?
Philip Marlowe in *The High Window* (1942), by Raymond Chandler.

In which mystery can the following line be found: "Ignorance may be bliss, but too often knowledge took the fun out of some parts of life"?
This line can be found in James Crumley's *Dancing Bear* (1983). The speaker is private investigator "Milo" Milodragovitch.

What detective offers this advice: "If anyone ever offers you a choice between luck and brains, take luck every time"?
This bit of wisdom comes from Matt Cobb in William DeAndrea's *Killed in the Ratings* (1978).

In what espionage thriller does this line appear: "There isn't a man, woman or child in this world who can say they have never conned someone out of something. Babies smile for a hug, girls for a mink, men for an empire"?
Only When I Larf (1968), by Len Deighton.

Questions of Character

Who was Mad Dog Earle?
Mad Dog Earle was the name of the character in W. R. Burnett's *High Sierra* (1940) who escapes from jail only to discover that his criminal ways and style are out of date. Humphrey Bogart played Mad Dog in the 1941 movie version.

What is the name of Margery Allingham's detective?
Albert Campion. He first appears in *The Crime at Black Dudley* (1929).

Who is Carlotta Carlyle?
She is the Boston-based, cab-driving detective created by Linda Barnes. Her first appearance in a novel is in *A Trouble of Fools* (1987). Before that, Carlotta was featured in the short story "Lucky Penny," which first appeared in *New Black Mask* (1986) and was later reprinted in the first *Sisters in Crime* anthology.

What is the name of Richard Barth's little-old-lady detective?
Margaret Binton. *The Rag Bag Clan* (1978) is the first book in the series.

What series features Hamish Macbeth?
Scottish detective Hamish Macbeth is the creation of M. C. Beaton. He first appears in *Death of a Gossip* (1985).

Who is Matthew Scudder?
He is the creation of Lawrence Block. Scudder is a recovering alcoholic and a former New York City cop who lives in a residential hotel in Midtown. He first appears in *In the Midst of Death* (1976).

What is the name of Michael Bond's gourmet-detective?
Monsieur Pamplemouse, who makes his debut in *Monsieur Pamplemouse* (1983).

Who is Doc Adams?
He is the oral surgeon and detective hero created by Rick Boyer. We meet Doc in *Billingsgate Shoal* (1982).

What is the name of James Lee Burke's Cajun detective?
Dave Robicheaux, who is a former New Orleans cop. He first appears in *Neon Rain* (1987).

Who is Miss Seeton?
She is a senior-citizen sleuth and the creation of Heron Carvic, who makes her debut in *Picture Miss Seeton* (1968).

What author created Dr. Gideon Fell?
John Dickson Carr. Fell first shows up in *Hag's Nook* (1933). Fell was a huge detective, weighing in at 250 pounds. In *The Man Who*

Could Not Shudder (1940), he is described as follows: "Vast and beaming, wearing a box-pleated cape as big as a tent, he sat . . . with his hands folded over his crutch stick. His shovel hat almost touched the canopy overhead. His eyeglasses were set precariously on a pink nose; the black ribbon of these glasses blew wide with each vast puff of breath which rumbled up from under his three chins, and agitated his bandit's moustache. But what you noticed most was the twinkle in his eye. A huge joy of life, a piratical swagger merely to be hearing and seeing and thinking, glowed from him like steam from a furnace. It was like meeting Old King Cole or Father Christmas."

What is the name of Raymond Chandler's detective?
Philip Marlowe, of course. Marlowe is first featured in *The Big Sleep* (1939).

What detective is known as "the warlord in the army of God"?
Uncle Abner, the creation of Melville Davisson Post, is often credited as the first great American detective. He lived in the America of Thomas Jefferson and was a very religious Virginian who saw himself as ordained by God to solve crime and dole out justice. See *Uncle Abner: Master of Mysteries* (1918).

What is the name of Amanda Cross's detective?
Professor Kate Fansler. She first appears in *In the Last Analysis* (1964).

Who is C. W. Sughrue?
He is the hard-drinking detective of *The Last Good Kiss* (1978), by James Crumley.

What is the name of Lindsey Davis's ancient Roman detective?
Marcus Didius Falco. He first appears in *Silver Pigs* (1989).

Who is Jill Smith?
She is one of Susan Dunlap's detectives, who makes her debut in *Karma* (1984).

What is the name of Loren Estleman's Detroit private investigator?
Amos Walker. He first appears in *Motor City Blues* (1981).

Who is Inspector Thomas Lynley?
He is Elizabeth George's detective. *A Great Deliverance* (1988) is the first in the series.

Who is Peter McGarr?
He is the police detective who debuts in *McGarr and the Politician's Wife* (1977), by Bartholomew Gill.

What is the name of Dorothy Gilman's series character?
She is Mrs. Emily Pollifax, a sweet, elderly spy, who first appears in *The Unexpected Mrs. Pollifax* (1966).

Who is the creator of Kinsey Millhone?
Kinsey Millhone is the detective in the wildly popular series created by Sue Grafton. She first appears in *"A" Is for Alibi* (1982).

What is the name of Stephen Greenleaf's San Francisco private investigator?
John Marshall Tanner. He makes his debut in *Grave Error* (1982).

Who is Richard Jury?
Superintendent Richard Jury of Scotland Yard is Martha Grimes's detective, who is first encountered in *The Man with a Load of Mischief* (1981).

What author writes about mystery bookstore owner Annie Laurance?
Carolyn Hart. Her first Annie Laurance book is *Death on Demand* (1987).

Who is John Cuddy, PI?
Cuddy is the Boston detective we first encounter in *Blunt Darts* (1984), by Jeremiah Healy.

What is the name of the character who runs the Book Depot?
That would be Joan Hess's Claire Malloy, who first appears in *Strangled Prose* (1986).

Who is Tom Ripley?
He is the creepy, yet fascinating, creation of Patricia Highsmith. Ripley makes his deadly debut in *The Talented Mr. Ripley* (1955).

What are the names of the two inspectors Reginald Hill writes about?
Superintendent Andrew Dalziel and Sergeant Pascoe, who are first encountered in *A Clubbable Woman* (1970).

What author writes about the Native American detectives Joe Leaphorn and Jim Chee?
Tony Hillerman. Leaphorn's first appearance is in *The Blessing Way* (1970) and we first meet Chee in *People of Darkness* (1980).

What is the name of P. D. James's inspector?
Commander Adam Dalgliesh. He first appears in *Cover Her Face* (1962).

What is the name of the Russian inspector who appears in Stuart Kaminsky's books?
Inspector Porfiry Rostnikov. He made his debut in *Rostnikov's Corpse* (1981).

Who writes about Rina Lazarus and Detective Peter Decker?
Faye Kellerman first wrote about this pair in *The Ritual Bath* (1985).

What author writes the series about child psychiatrist Alex Delaware?
Jonathan Kellerman. Delaware first appears in *When the Bough Breaks* (1985).

Who is Kat Colorado?
She is the creation of Karen Kijewski. Kat makes her debut in *Katwalk* (1989).

What is the name of Jane Langton's detective?
His name is Homer Kelly and he first appears in *The Transcendental Murder* (1964).

Who is Easy Rawlins?
Easy Rawlins is a black detective who works out of Los Angeles and first appears in *Devil in a Blue Dress* (1990). The author is Walter Mosley.

What is the name of the female private investigator who works in Chicago?
V. I. Warshawski. She made her debut in *Indemnity Only* (1982), by Sara Paretsky.

What is the name of the author who created Spenser?
Robert B. Parker. He first introduces Spenser in *The Godwulf Manuscript* (1973).

Who is Sharon McCone?
She is Marcia Muller's detective. McCone, who is often credited as being the first of the hard-boiled female detectives, makes her first appearance in *Edwin of the Iron Shoes* (1977).

What is the name of Elizabeth Peters's archaeologist detective?
Amelia Peabody Emerson. This series is set in Victorian Britain as well as Egypt, and Amelia makes her debut in *Crocodile on the Sandbank* (1975).

What is the name of the twelfth-century Benedictine monk detective?
Ellis Peters's character Brother Cadfael, who first appears in *A Morbid Taste of Bones* (1977).

To which author does Inspector Wexford belong?
Ruth Rendell. She introduces Wexford in *From Doon with Death* (1964).

What is the name of the Philadelphia schoolteacher detective?
Amanda Pepper. She first appears in *Caught Dead in Philadelphia* (1987), by Gillian Roberts.

Who is Inspector Alan Banks?
He is the creation of Peter Robinson. Banks makes his debut in *Gallows View* (1987).

Who is the creator of Lord Peter Wimsey?

Dorothy L. Sayers, who introduced Wimsey in *Whose Body* (1923).

Who is Inspector Maigret?
He is the creation of Georges Simenon. Maigret makes his debut in
The Death of Monsieur Gallet (1932).

**What author writes about Officer Skip Langdon of the New
Orleans Police Department?**
Julie Smith, who introduces Skip in the Edgar Award–winning
New Orleans Mourning (1990).

What is the name of Mickey Spillane's detective?
Mike Hammer. He first appears in *I, The Jury* (1947).

Who is Nero Wolfe?
He is the creation of Rex Stout. Wolfe makes his debut in *Fer-de-
Lance* (1934).

What author writes about Boston lawyer Brady Coyne?
William G. Tapply, who introduced Coyne in *Death at Charity's
Point* (1984).

**What is the name of Andrew Vachss's renegade and under-
ground detective?**
Burke, who first appears in *Flood* (1985).

Who is Hoke Moseley?
He is Charles Willeford's detective, who first appears in *Miami
Blues* (1984).

Who is Inspector Charlie Salter?

He is a Toronto policeman, the creation of Eric Wright. Salter makes his first appearance in *The Night the Gods Smiled* (1983).

Who is Dr. Nikola?
He is the unscrupulous and ruthless creation of Guy Boothby. We meet Dr. Nikola, an evil genius and talented hypnotist, in *The Lust of Hate* (1898).

What is the name of the Dorothy Dunnett character who is a portrait painter and sails his own yacht, *Dolly*?
Johnson Johnson. The books are funny, fast-paced thrillers, and the first in the series is *Dolly and the Singing Bird* (1968).

What is the name of the "skeleton detective"—you know, the guy sort of like Quincy?
That would be Aaron Elkins's protagonist, Gideon Oliver, who is a professor of physical anthropology. The first book in this excellent series is *Fellowship of Fear* (1982).

What is Inspector Maigret's first name?
Jules is the first name of Georges Simenon's brilliantly conceived inspector, who first appears in *The Death of Monsieur Gallet* (1932) and makes his final appearance in *The Rules of the Game* (1989). Simenon died in 1989.

Who is the "Hairless Mexican"?
He is a friend of Ashenden's as well as a hired assassin, who appears in W. Somerset Maugham's *Ashenden* (1928). His advice is never to play cards with strangers.

Who is Kenyatta?
Crime fiction's first black revolutionary series hero, Kenyatta is the creation of Donald Goines. He first appears in *Crime Partners* (1974).

Who is Encyclopedia Brown?

He is the creation of Donald Sobol. One of the most popular child detectives, Master Brown is about ten years old and runs his own detective agency; on tricky cases he consults with his father, a police officer. See *Encyclopedia Brown Boy Detective* (1963).

Who is "Beau" Pepys?

He is one of Gerald Hammond's detectives. Pepys, an architect and race car driver, first appears in *Fred in Situ* (1965).

Who is Dave Brandstetter?

He is Joseph Hansen's gay detective, who first appears in *Fadeout* (1970). It took three years for Hansen to find a publisher brave enough to accept his nonapologetic approach to a taboo subject. Luckily, mystery editor Joan Kahn of Harper & Row liked Hansen's work and agreed to publish the series.

"Private Snoop—Medical/Health Matters Only." What detective does this refer to?

Edwina Crusoe, R.N., who is a highly paid private nurse and medical consultant. Try *Fatal Diagnosis* (1990), by Mary Kittridge.

Who is Blanche White?

She is a forty-year-old African-American who works as a domestic in North Carolina, where she investigates a murder she is afraid will be blamed on her. Blanche White made her impressive debut in *Blanche on the Lam* (1992) and is the creation of Barbara Neely.

What detective of the early 1900s described himself as "the best detective in New York"?

"Fatty" Welch, a man of many faces, appears in a series of stories ("The Escape of Wilkins," 1905) written by the lawyer-author Arthur Train.

Which of the early "hard-boiled dicks" was said to have increased magazine sales by 20 percent just by having his name on the cover?

Race Williams, the wisecracking creation of Carroll John Daly. Race first appeared in *Black Mask* magazine in the 1920s.

How many novels does Dashiell Hammett's detective Sam Spade appear in?

Only one, *The Maltese Falcon* (1930).

What private investigator got a job guarding wedding presents on an island?

Dashiell Hammett's nameless detective, the Continental Op. In a classic scene where the lights go out and a gang starts looting the island's homes and businesses, the Op becomes wounded and "borrows" a cane. When he comes face to face with a woman in the gang, she refuses to believe he will shoot her and tries to make her escape, when "I put a bullet in the calf of her left leg. She sat down—plump! Utter surprise stretched her white face. It was too soon for pain. . . . 'You ought to have known I'd do it!' My voice sounded harsh and savage and like a stranger's in my ears. 'Didn't I steal a crutch from a cripple?' "

What did Raymond Chandler's character Philip Marlowe think about Ernest Hemingway?

Not much. In *Farewell, My Lovely* (1940) Marlowe keeps calling a crooked cop Hemingway. The cop finally asks, "Who is this Hemingway person at all?" Marlowe, who has just been beaten up answers, "A guy that keeps saying the same thing over and over until you begin to believe it must be good."

How did Rex Stout come up with his character, Nero Wolfe?

Stout refused to ever talk about this subject.

The Writers

What sort of work did Elmore Leonard do before he became a full-time writer?
Elmore Leonard was a copywriter for Campbell Ewald advertising agency in Detroit (1950–61); a writer of industrial and educational films (1961–63); and finally the Director of Elmore Leonard Advertising Company (1963–66). He didn't begin writing full-time until 1967, when, at the age of forty-two, he had already published five westerns and several short stories. After two more westerns, several screenplays and a dozen mysteries, he hit the best-seller lists in 1985 with the publication of *Glitz*.

Note: One of the last projects Alfred Hitchcock worked on before he died in 1980 was a film adaptation of Leonard's *Unknown Man No. 89*. The screenplay was never finished and the film was never made.

How does Dick Francis know so much about the world of horses?
Dick Francis was one of the best steeplechase riders of all time, becoming champion jockey in 1954 and racing under the Queen

Mother's colors for four years. In the 1956 Grand National he had a ten-length lead when his horse, Devon Loch, collapsed in the stretch. When Francis retired in 1957, he had run in 2,305 races, compiling a record of 345 wins, 285 seconds, and 240 thirds. According to Mr. Francis, the inspiration to write his first mystery came when his wife wanted a new carpet and they didn't have enough money; his first book, *Dead Cert,* came out in 1962 and was an instant success.

What does the "P. D." in P. D. James stand for?
Phyllis Dorothy. This author of British police procedurals is so well loved and respected that in 1983 she was appointed Officer, Order of the British Empire.

What well-known and prolific science fiction author also wrote mysteries?
Isaac Asimov wrote seven mysteries (including *Murder at the ABA,* 1976) and seven collections of mystery stories, in addition to more than three hundred other books, most of which were science fiction.

Has any mystery author created a character he couldn't stand?
Several authors have ended a series by killing off their detective— even Arthur Conan Doyle tried killing Sherlock Holmes, but the public wouldn't let him. Anthony Berkeley said about his character, Roger Sheringham, that he was "founded on an offensive person I once knew because, in my original innocence, I thought it would be amusing to have an offensive detective. Since he has been taken in all seriousness, I have had to tone his offensiveness down and pretend he never was."

What writer of crime fiction explains his work by saying that he is the bastard child of Raymond Chandler?
James Crumley is known to have made such a comment. He has also said that while he is definitely influenced by Chandler, his de-

tectives don't share Philip Marlowe's sense of morality—the sixties
and Vietnam changed things too much for that. See *The Last Good
Kiss* (1978).

What mystery writer was Raymond Chandler's London solicitor?
Michael Gilbert, who published his first mystery, *Close Quarters*, in
1947 and is still writing today.

What British mystery writer thinks of himself as writing science fiction with the science left out?
Peter Dickinson. He says, "I try to write proper detective stories,
with clues and solutions, which work in the traditional way, but
also provide something extra by way of ideas, without getting portentous about it." Dickinson's gift is his ability to create fascinating
and believable worlds. *Try Sleep and His Brother* (1971).

What is the name of the author of the series set in Saratoga? Isn't he also a well-known poet?
Stephen Dobyns, in addition to being a respected poet, also writes
detective books set in Saratoga, New York, featuring Charlie Bradshaw. The first in the series is *Saratoga Longshot* (1978).

Didn't the author of *To Catch a Thief* (1952) start out writing mysteries about a tax accountant?
Yes. David Dodge's first four books featured Whit Whitney, a tax
accountant and reluctant investigator. The first in the series is
Death and Taxes (1941), and all four are in the screwball style of
Dashiell Hammett's *The Thin Man* (1934).

Are there any mystery writers who are married to each other?
Here are four such couples: Margaret Millar (*Beast in View*, 1955)
and Ross Macdonald (*The Chill*, 1964); William L. DeAndrea

(*Killed in the Ratings,* 1978) and Orania Papazoglou (*Sweet Savage Death,* 1984); Marcia Muller (*Ask the Cards a Question,* 1982) and Bill Pronzini (*Dragonfire,* 1982); and Jonathan (*When the Bough Breaks,* 1985) and Faye Kellerman (*The Ritual Bath,* 1985).

What well-known writer of hard-boiled detective fiction also wrote *A Guide Book to Australian Coins* (1965)?
Lawrence Block, the creator of private eye Matt Scudder (*Eight Million Ways to Die,* 1982) and burglar Bernie Rhodenbarr (*Burglars Can't Be Choosers,* 1977).

When was Erle Stanley Gardner born?
He was born on July 17, 1889, in Malden, Massachusetts. He gave up a lucrative law practice in 1933 to write crime fiction full time, and that same year published his first novel, *The Case of the Velvet Claws.* It was the first of eighty-two Perry Mason books.

Which mystery writer of dubious talent liked to call his books "shockers"?
Sydney Horler, the author of nearly one hundred novels. (We can't imagine anyone reading them all, but it's safe to say that they are all pretty bad). He himself once said, "I know I haven't the brains to write a proper detective novel, but there is no class of literature for which I feel a deeper personal loathing."

What well-known author of hard-boiled detective fiction began to write after losing his job as an oil company executive?
Raymond Chandler, author of such classics as *The Big Sleep* (1939) and *The Lady in the Lake* (1943).

What author was inspired to start writing mysteries after reading Dashiell Hammett stories while he was in prison?
Chester Himes, who wrote about the urban black experience of the

late sixties. His main characters are Harlem detectives Grave Digger Jones and Coffin Ed Johnson. See *Cotton Comes to Harlem* (1965).

What British mystery author also happens to be the creator of Paddington the Bear?
Michael Bond, the author of the Monsieur Pamplemousse series.

Which mystery writers did Raymond Chandler like to read?
Someone once asked him who was the "best mystery writer" and he replied, "Can't answer, too many types. By sales Gardner and Christie. Can't read Christie, Gardner close personal friend. Carter Dickinson I can't read but others love him. . . . This is a lot of nonsense. You have to agree on definitions and standards."

What mystery author went to prison during the witch hunt of the fifties because he refused to name names of a Communist front organization?
Dashiell Hammett (*The Maltese Falcon,* 1930), who was probably, though not certainly, a card-carrying Communist. Hammett told the Supreme Court that "Communism to me is not a dirty word."

What mystery author worked on the scripts of two Stanley Kubrick films, *The Killing* and *Paths of Glory*?
Jim Thompson, one of the darkest practitioners of the noir school. His best books are *The Killer Inside Me* (1952) and *Pop. 1280* (1964).
    Note: A copy of the paperback original *Killer Inside Me* in mint condition currently fetches somewhere between $800 and $1,000 on the collector's market.

Who was the philosopher Ludwig Wittgenstein's favorite mystery author?
Norbert Davis (*Dead Little Rich Girl,* 1945), a writer of the hard-boiled school.

What author answered the question, "How do you write mysteries?" by saying, "How you write 'em is write 'em"?

James M. Cain, the author of nineteen crime novels, including *The Postman Always Rings Twice* (1934) and *Double Indemnity* (1944).

Have any mystery authors written more than five hundred books?

Yes. John Creasey and Nicholas Carter both have, but Carter was more than one person—it was the "house name" assigned to whoever was responsible at the time for the exploits of the character Nick Carter. It looks as if Creasey is in no danger of being dethroned as the king of sheer bulk, with 560 titles; his bibliography takes up ten very large pages in *The 20th-Century Crime & Mystery Writers*.

Colorful and original language is often used by hard-boiled detectives like Sam Spade and Philip Marlowe. Did any authors go completely overboard in terms of descriptive language?

Robert Leslie Bellem was the worst offender in terms of hard-boiledese. His character Dan Turner never uses a simple word if he can find a more dreadful one: women became "cupcakes" and "wrens"; cigarettes, "gaspers"; breasts, "whatchacallems" and "thingumbobs"; and guns, "rodneys" and "roscoes." He once referred to a corpse as "dead as a cannibal's conscience."

Did Raymond Chandler write an essay in which he blasted British mystery writers for being trite and unrealistic?

In 1944 Chandler wrote the essay "The Simple Art of Murder" in response to the English country house school of mystery writing. In it he wrote that Dashiell Hammett "gave murder back to the kind of people that commit it for reasons, not just to provide a corpse; and with the means at hand, not with hand-wrought dueling pistols, curare, and tropical fish."

Who was the mystery writer who always put a color in his titles?
John D. MacDonald put a different color in each of his mysteries featuring Travis McGee, from *The Deep Blue Goodbye* (1964) to *The Lonely Silver Rain* (1985). Walter Mosley is also working on a color theme, with *Devil in a Blue Dress* (1990), *A Red Death* (1991), *White Butterfly* (1992), and *Black Betty* (1994).

What suspense author said, "Criminals are dramatically interesting, because for a time at least they are active, free in spirit, and they do not knuckle down to anyone. . . . I find the public passion for justice quite boring and artificial, for neither life nor nature cares if justice is ever done or not"?
Patricia Highsmith, cited in *Bloody Murder* (2nd ed., 1993), by Julian Symons.

What was James Lee Burke's first book?
Most people know James Lee Burke for his recently popular detective series (*The Neon Rain*, 1987; *Heaven's Prisoners*, 1988; *Black Cherry Blues*, 1989; etc.) featuring a former New Orleans cop, Dave Robicheaux, but Burke has also written several excellent nonmysteries, the first of which was *Half of Paradise* (1965). He received much critical acclaim but little financial success until he started writing mysteries at the suggestion of his friend and mentor, Charles Willeford.

Is it true that Fredric Brown wrote science fiction as well as detective stories?
Brown wrote such science fiction classics as *Martians, Go Home* (1955) and *What Mad Universe* (1949). He said that he occasionally wrote science fiction because he found that detective fiction was "too real."

What was Cornell Woolrich's first book?
The Bride Wore Black (1940). It features a grief-crazed woman who

assumes several identities to enter the lives of five different men, whom she kills one by one while a homicide detective stalks her.

What mystery author had a theory that people who didn't like mysteries were anarchists?
Rex Stout, the creator of Nero Wolfe. He also liked to say that reading mysteries was more fun than writing them.

Didn't another author say that mysteries are too easy?
In *The Three Hostages* (1924) John Buchan had a character say, "These shockers are too easy. . . . The author writes the story inductively, and the reader follows it deductively."

How much was Robert B. Parker paid to finish writing *Poodle Springs* (1989), the uncompleted Raymond Chandler manuscript?
Reportedly $1 million. Parker is best known for being the creator of the Boston detective Spenser (see *God Save the Child*, 1974).

Who is the sort of eccentric and sometimes caustic country-western singer who also writes mysteries?
That would be Kinky Friedman, who not only writes mysteries but also stars in them as the detective. The books are wacky, but it's obvious Kinky has read a heap of mysteries and knows what he's doing. Try *Greenwich Killing Time* (1986).

How did Rex Stout make his fortune?
He invented a school banking system. He was in his late forties and financially established when he wrote the first Nero Wolfe book, *Fer-de-Lance* (1934).

Didn't Agatha Christie disappear sometime in the 1920s?
She did, in 1926, disappear from her home in Sunningdale, and

the police searched for her for more than a week before it was learned she was at the Hydropathic Hotel in North Yorkshire. The whole story is still unclear.

What is the name of the well-known post–Depression era poet who wrote the suspense classic *The Big Clock* (1946)?
Kenneth Fearing. *The Big Clock* is a masterpiece of subtle and complex characterization, as well as a brilliant study in the use of multiple and recurrent narrators.

Of which mystery writer is it said that he acquired his deep feeling for tragedy from seeing a performance of Puccini's opera *Madama Butterfly* when he was eight years old?
Cornell Woolrich, who was never a happy man. Six of his books have the word "black" in the title and three others contain the word "darkness": *The Bride Wore Black*, 1940; *The Black Curtain*, 1941; *Black Alibi*, 1942; *The Black Angel*, 1943; *The Black Path of Fear*, 1944; *Rendezvous in Black*, 1948; *Waltz Into Darkness*, 1947; *Angels of Darkness*, 1979; *Darkness at Dawn*, 1985.

What author once said that the "ideal mystery" was "one you would read if the end was missing"?
Raymond Chandler, author of *The Little Sister* (1949) and *The Long Goodbye* (1953).

And who said, "You don't read a book to get to the middle. You read it to get to the end"?
Mickey Spillane, author of *I, The Jury* (1947) and *My Gun Is Quick* (1950).

Which hugely prolific mystery writer was expelled from college for slugging a professor?
Erle Stanley Gardner, the creator of Perry Mason, who wrote eighty-two mysteries, including *The Case of the Velvet Claws* (1933).

What very successful British mystery author has now written a novel that is more science fiction than it is mystery?
P. D. James. Her latest book, *The Children of Men* (1993), is set in the year 2021 with the human race coming to an end, because since 1995 all males have been infertile.

What mystery author once said, "Writing is not a profession but a vocation of unhappiness"?
Georges Simenon, creator of Inspector Maigret, during an interview for *Writers at Work: First Series.*

How much formal education did Dashiell Hammett receive?
He was educated at the Baltimore Polytechnic Institute until he was thirteen years old.

What sort of work did Thomas Harris do before he became a successful author?
He worked as a news reporter and editor for the Associated Press in New York City before going on to write such well-known books as *The Silence of the Lambs* (1988).

What crime author did Graham Greene call "a poet of apprehension"?
He said that of Patricia Highsmith, the author of *Strangers on a Train* (1950) and the creator of Tom Ripley, the creepy-yet-likable title character of *The Talented Mr. Ripley* (1955).

Whom did Graham Greene call "the greatest living writer of the novel of suspense"?
Eric Ambler, the author of *A Coffin for Dimitrios* (1939).

Has any mystery writer ever commented on why murder is so popular a crime in fiction?

Dorothy L. Sayers once wrote, "Death in particular seems to provide the minds of the Anglo-Saxon race with a greater fund of innocent amusement than any other single subject . . . Let the murder turn out to be no murder, but a mere accident or suicide, and letters pour in from indignant readers. . . . The tale must be about dead bodies or very wicked people, preferably both, before the Tired Business Man can feel really happy and be at peace with the world."

Didn't Edgar Allan Poe marry his own very young cousin?
In 1836 Poe married his fourteen-year-old cousin, Virginia Clemm. At the time Poe was twenty-seven years old.

Did they live happily ever after?
Not exactly. Virginia died in 1847 of tuberculosis. Poe was rootless, penniless, and often drunk. One young woman promised to marry him if he would stop drinking, but instead Poe courted a married woman until he met a childhood sweetheart to whom he proposed. When she accepted, he set off on another drunken binge which landed him in jail. Soon after, on November 15, 1849, after a violent attack of delirium tremens, he died in the hospital. He was forty years old.

What real-life former bartender now writes a detective series which features an ex-bartender turned private investigator?
Karen Kijewski, who writes about Kat Colorado, a private investigator in Sacramento, California. Kat debuts in *Katapult* (1990).

What well-known mystery author died during the sinking of the *Titanic*?
Jacques Futrelle, the creator of the eccentric Professor Augustus S. F. X. Van Dusen, who was also known as the "the Thinking Machine." Futrelle was able to save his wife and daughter, but he himself did not survive. See *The Problem of Cell 13* (1918).

What writer of detective stories was a long-time court reporter?
Roy Vickers, who created "The Department of Dead Ends," a small division of Scotland Yard men assigned to impossible cases. One of the best of these tales is "The Starting Handle Murder" (1934).

What mystery author once said, "Detective stories are a harmless release of an innate spring of cruelty present in everyone"?
Nicholas Blake (a pseudonym of Cecil Day-Lewis). Blake wrote such classics as *The Beast Must Die* (1938) and *Head of a Traveler* (1949).

What mystery author taught a mystery-writing class in New York City for a decade after World War II?
Dashiell Hammett. One of his students told Hammett biographer William F. Nolan, "He taught us that tempo is the vital thing in fiction, and that you've got to keep things moving, and character can be drawn within the action."

What mystery author wrote his doctoral dissertation on the early nineteenth-century English poet Samuel Taylor Coleridge?
Ross Macdonald, the creator of Lew Archer, earned his doctorate degree from the University of Michigan in 1951. Archer first appears in *The Moving Target* (1949).

Were Raymond Chandler and Dashiell Hammett friends?
As far as we can tell, they met only once at a dinner party on January 11, 1936. They hardly spoke, only exchanging pleasantries.

When Rex Stout met Mark Twain, what did they talk about?
When Stout met Twain in 1909 they talked about one of Twain's obsessions, copyright law. It turns out that Twain was convinced that his publishers were always trying to cheat him.

What was the dollar amount of the publisher's advance paid to Robert Bloch for *Psycho* (1959)?
It was $750.00. After his agent took his 10 percent, Bloch received $675.00.

Pseudonyms

What mystery author has written under the most pseudonyms?
John Creasey has written under at least twenty-four different names. They include: Gordon Ashe, M. E. Cooke, Margaret Cooke, Henry St. John Cooper, Norman Deane, Elise Fecamps, Robert Caine Frazer, Patric Gill, Michael Halliday, Charles Hogarth, Brian Hope, Colin Hughes, Kyle Hunt, Abel Mann, Peter Manton, J. J. Marric, James Marsden, Richard Martin, Rodney Mattheson, Anthony Morton, Ken Ranger, William K. Reilly, Tex Reilly, and Jeremy York.

Is it true that Ellery Queen was really two people?
Yes, but a complete answer is tricky, so hang on. Ellery Queen is the pseudonym of a pair of Brooklyn-born cousins named Frederic Dannay and Manfred Lee, although they were born Daniel Nathan and Manford Lepofsky, respectively. To make matters even more complicated, they named their fictional detective Ellery Queen. They also wrote under the pseudonym Barnaby Ross.
Note: A true Ellery Queen "signature" can be identified by two

strokes in the letter "Q"—this touch being a nod to their two-in-one author package.

What famous—and outspoken—novelist and critic wrote mysteries under the pseudonym Edgar Box?
Gore Vidal wrote three mysteries in the early fifties: *Death in the Fifth Position* (1952), *Death Before Bedtime* (1953), and *Death Likes It Hot* (1954).

Who is the only detective story writer to have been England's Poet Laureate?
Cecil Day-Lewis, who was named the Poet Laureate in 1968, wrote twenty detective novels under the name of Nicholas Blake. His detective, Nigel Strangeways—an Oxford graduate with many skills but no real profession—appears in sixteen mysteries, including *A Question of Proof* (1935).

What is the real name of Jack Higgins?
Henry Patterson writes as Jack Higgins, whose best known book is *The Eagle Has Landed* (1975).

What was the real name of Geoffrey Homes, the author of Build My Gallows High (1946)?
His real name is Daniel Mainwaring, and he also adapted Jack Finney's *The Body Snatcher* (1955) into the science fiction film classic, *The Invasion of the Body Snatchers* (1956).

What pair of twin brothers writes under the pseudonym of Peter Antony?
Anthony and Peter Shaffer. Yes, *the* Peter Shaffer, the playwright who wrote *Equus* and *Amadeus*. Anthony Shaffer is the author of the wonderful *Sleuth* (1970) and the screenwriter for a number of mystery films including Hitchcock's *Frenzy*. Together, the brothers wrote three crime novels, all of them featuring a detective named

Mr. Verity (who is inexplicably renamed Fathom in the last book). Verity is "an immense man, just tall enough to carry his breadth majestically." He often wore a huge purple bathing costume which he bought in 1924 from a fruit merchant in Beirut. The Shaffers' first mystery, *The Woman in the Wardrobe* (1951), is their finest and perhaps the best locked-room mystery written in the last forty years.

Which half of a famous writing team said of his partner: "[He] can't be troubled with description and narrative, and I'm no good at creating characters or dialogue?"
That was Hilary Aidan St. George Saunders, speaking of John Leslie Palmer. The two of them shared a pair of pseudonyms, Francis Beeding and David Pilgrim, and together they produced some fifty detective novels and thrillers. The best is the classic *Death Walks in Eastrepps* (1931).

Under what pseudonym did the author Howard Fast write mysteries?
Howard Fast wrote mysteries under the name E. V. Cunningham, producing some twenty-three titles, including *The Case of the Poisoned Eclairs* (1979). Under his own name he wrote thirty-five novels.

What is the real name of the author who wrote under the names Murdo Coombs, Stephen Ransome, and Curtis Steele, as well as his own name?
Frederick C. Davis wrote more than one thousand stories for the pulps and forty-eight novels under his own name and the three pseudonyms. Davis had a real knack for coming up with a catchy title—*Another Morgue Heard From* (1954), *Poor, Poor Yorick* (1939), *He Wouldn't Stay Dead* (1939).

What pseudonym did Joyce Emmerson Preston Muddock write under?

With a name like that you have to wonder why a fellow would ever take a pseudonym, but Joyce Emmerson Preston Muddock did, writing under the less weighty, albeit also less regal, name of Dick Donovan. He wrote thirty full-length mysteries and over two hundred short stories between 1886 and 1922. Try *From the Bosom of the Deep* (1886).

What was Ed Lacy's real name?
Len Zinberg. Lacy was the creator of black detective Toussaint Moore, protagonist of the Edgar Award–winning *Room to Swing* (1957).

What was Patricia Wentworth's real name?
Her real name was Dora Amy Elles Dillon Turnbull, and she was the creator of the lovable and genteel Miss Silver, who made her debut in *The Case Is Closed* (1937).

What was Craig Rice's real name?
Georgiana Ann Randolph. Her best character was the drunken lawyer John J. Malone, who was quicker with a cliché than a gun. Try *The Corpse Steps Out* (1940).

Is it true that Barbara Michaels is also Elizabeth Peters?
Barbara Michaels and Elizabeth Peters are both pseudonyms for Barbara G. Mertz, who writes popular nonfiction on Egyptology under her own name. As Barbara Michaels, she generally features historical backgrounds with a mildly supernatural atmosphere (including *The Walker in Shadows*, 1979); as Peters she writes mysteries dealing with art and archaeology (*The Last Camel Died at Noon*, 1992).

What is Ellis Peters's real name?
Edith Mary Pargeter. As Peters, she is most known for the creation of Brother Cadfael, monk detective, who debuts in *A Morbid Taste*

for Bones (1977). Under her own name she has written over thirty books, mostly historical novels.

What other names did Cornell Woolrich write under?

William Irish (*I Married a Dead Man*, 1948) and George Hopley (*Night Has a Thousand Eyes*, 1945).

What is Michael Innes's real name?

John Innes Mackintosh Stewart. Innes's detective is Inspector John Appleby, a good-mannered, erudite policeman. Appleby first appears in *Death at the President's Lodging* (1936).

What is John le Carré's real name?

David John Moore Cornwell. As le Carré, he is best known for his complex and literary espionage novels featuring George Smiley. Try *The Spy Who Came in from the Cold* (1963).

What is the real name of Eugène Sue?

Marie Joseph Sue. His four-volume work *Les Mystères de Paris* was published in the 1840s.

Who is Kenneth Millar?

Author of the Lew Archer series (first book, *The Moving Target*, 1949), Kenneth Millar is the real name of Ross Macdonald. After his wife, Margaret Millar, published her first mystery, he also began to write, published four books under his own name, and decided to write under the name of John Ross Macdonald to avoid being confused with his wife. Then people confused him with John D. MacDonald, so he changed his name to Ross Macdonald.

What is Anthony Gilbert's real name?

Lucy Beatrice Malleson. Although she is best known as Anthony Gilbert, she also wrote under the pseudonyms J. Kilmeny Keity and Anne Meredith. Her most famous character is lawyer-detective Arthur G. Crook, who is addicted to bright brown off-the-rack suits. Crook debuts in *Murder by Experts* (1936).

What is Dell Shannon's real name?

Elizabeth Linington, who also wrote as Anne Blaisdell, Lesley Egan, and Egan O'Neill. Shannon is best known as the creator of Lieutenant Luis Mendoza, who debuts in *Case Pending* (1960).

Espionage and
Thrillers

What sort of gun does James Bond carry?
In Ian Fleming's first five Bond novels, Bond's main weapon is a
.25-caliber Beretta, and his backup gun is an unspecified Colt .45
revolver. From *Dr. No* on, Bond carries a Walther PPK, having
abandoned the Beretta—which had jammed in a gunfight—and he
also trades in the Colt for a Smith & Wesson .38 Centennial Air-
weight. Bond uses these guns in seven more novels and eight short
stories.

**What warning did R., chief of Intelligence for the British se-
cret service, give to Ashenden before adding him to the staff?**
"If you do well you'll get no thanks, and if you get into trouble
you'll get no help." The book is W. Somerset Maugham's *Ashenden*
(1928).

**What suspense novelist has a knack for turning captor-captive
situations into love affairs?**
Evelyn Anthony. Eventual lovers in her books can be instantly

identified by the strong and immutable sexual attraction they feel for each other at inappropriate moments. In *The Persian Ransom* (1973) a kidnapping victim and one of her captors fall in love, while in *Rendezvous* (1967), a former Nazi falls in love with a woman he had interrogated during the war; she remembers the experience with terror, but loves him anyway.

What thriller features a Russian military training camp that turns out spies entirely versed in Americana?
Nelson Demille's *The Charm School* (1988). An American tourist on a driving tour of Russia picks up a man who claims to have spent twenty years in "Mrs. Ivanova's Charm School."

In what adventure-thriller must a former Yalie save Algeria from dastardly archvillains?
Edward S. Aarons's *Assignment—Madeleine* (1958). The Yalie is Sam Durell, a member of the CIA "K" section. He appears in forty-one "Assignment" books and is always saving some country or other and getting the girl.

In what espionage novel is a fourteen-year-old boy with total recall recruited by British Intelligence as a spy?
Victor Canning's *The Boy on Platform One* (1981) employs this device. The boy's job is to listen to (and remember, of course) a list of spies as recited by a French count.

What is Goldfinger's first name?
Ian Fleming, often the joker, gave Goldfinger—one of James Bond's deadliest foes—the first name of Auric.

What fictional freelance American agent has the occupational classification of "Nullifier"?
Philip Atlee's Joe Gall is a contract killer who is called to action when a timely death is in the best interest of America. The first Joe

Gall book was *The Death Bird Contract* (1966).

What was Mr. Moto's first name?
Mr. Moto was Japan's number one secret agent (debut: *Ming Yellow*, 1935) who could do many things, speak many languages, and kill a man without blinking. We don't ever learn his first name, only the initials I.O. In a 1959 interview Mr. Moto's creator, John P. Marquand, said, "Mr. Moto was my literary disgrace. I wrote about him to get shoes for the baby. I can't say why people still remember him."

What British spy is afraid of airplanes and gets woozy at the sight of blood?
John Gardner's Boysie Oakes of Britain's Department of Special Security. See *Understrike* (1965).

What secret agent is described by his wife as "breathtakingly ordinary"?
Lady Ann Sercomb says that about her husband, George Smiley, who is quiet, bespectacled, and a scholar in obscure German poets. Smiley and his wife are the creations of John le Carré who make their first appearance in *Call for the Dead* (1962).

Did James Bond ever marry?
He considered marrying several times but only made it to the altar once, in *On Her Majesty's Secret Service* (1963). He married Teresa (Tracy) Di Vicenzo, who was killed about an hour later by the evil Blofeld.

What author of thrillers writes about a character with the unlikely name Dirk Pitt?
Clive Cussler. Dirk Pitt has appeared in seven thrillers, the most famous of which is *Raise the Titanic* (1977). Pitt is the son of a congressman, an ex–Air Force pilot, and the Special Projects Director

of the National Underwater and Marine Agency.

What espionage author won critical acclaim in 1960 for his remarkably vivid thriller set in Czechoslovakia, which he wrote without ever having visited the country?
Lionel Davidson apparently did good research. His first book, *The Night of Wenceslas* (1960) was hailed for its sharp and vivid portrayal of Czechoslovakia.

What well-known, best-selling thriller writer used to write action/adventure police novels?
Before Nelson DeMille made it big with blockbusters·such as *The Charm School* (1988), he wrote seven cop books featuring tough cops in a tough world. The first of them is *The Sniper* (1974).

What espionage writer actually spent ten years working for the CIA?
Charles McCarry. McCarry is the creator of poet-spy Paul Christopher, who first appears in the excellent novel *The Miernik Dossier* (1973).

Has there ever been a spy writer who used to be a British Intelligence agent?
John le Carré was indeed an agent. By the way, *Time* called this spy writer "the premier novelist of his time." Try *The Spy Who Came in from the Cold* (1963).

What counterspy went by the code name "Eric"?
Matt Helm, a character created by Donald Hamilton.

What thriller, written in 1939, tells the story of a British aristocrat who attempts to assassinate the dictator of a Central European country?

Geoffrey Household's *Rogue Male*. On the matter of obviously writing about Adolf Hitler, Household said, "Something had to be done about the man, and I started thinking about how I would love to kill him."

What collection of spy stories did Anthony Boucher, critic for *The New York Times*, consider to be the best ever published?
Ashenden (1928), by W. Somerset Maugham. Boucher thought Michael Gilbert's *Game Without Rules* (1967) was second best.

In espionage thrillers someone is always hiding information in a microdot. What, exactly, is a microdot?
The Nazis have been credited with inventing microdot technology, which reduces a printed page some 250 times, to the size of the head of a pin. The microdot would then be added to the dotted pattern of an envelope or worn as a beauty mark or otherwise concealed somewhere in plain sight. When the dot reaches its destination it can then be enlarged to a readable size.

What writer of spy novels is a former Eton master?
John le Carré (a pseudonym for David Cornwell). He is arguably the most successful author in the genre after Ian Fleming.

Politics and Murder

Who is President Clinton's favorite mystery writer?
Currently it's Walter Mosley, whose mysteries *Devil in a Blue Dress* (1990), *Red Death* (1991), *White Butterfly* (1992), and *Black Betty* (1994), feature Easy Rawlins, a black World War II veteran. The setting is Los Angeles in the 1940s and 1950s, and while Easy isn't exactly a private investigator, he becomes known in the black community as a man who can solve problems and find answers.

President Clinton is also known to favor the authors Ross Thomas, an excellent writer of thrillers (usually involving some sort of scam and set against a backdrop of insider political intrigue), and Sara Paretsky, who writes about V. I. Warshawski, a hard-boiled female private eye based in Chicago.

Have any other political figures enjoyed mysteries?
Many political figures have appreciated the genre. Abraham Lincoln, Franklin Delano Roosevelt, John F. Kennedy, Henry Kissinger, Julian Bond, and Amy Carter have all admitted to being hooked on them. Gordon Liddy of the Nixon Administration has not only written mysteries but also lived through a few.

Who was John F. Kennedy's favorite mystery writer?

He claimed that his favorite writer was Ian Fleming, the creator of James Bond.

Is it true that F.D.R. wrote a mystery?

Yes and no—he had an idea for one, but couldn't come up with a good ending. Six authors came to his rescue: Anthony Abbot, Rupert Hughes, S. H. Adams, Rita Weiman, S. S. Van Dine, and John Erskine. Each wrote a chapter and more or less resolved the problem of absconding with $5 million without leaving any clues. Originally published as *The President's Mystery Story* (1935), it was later reprinted as *The President's Mystery Plot* (1967) with a final chapter by Erle Stanley Gardner.

What conservative spokesman and editor of the *National Review* is also the author of best-selling spy novels?

William F. Buckley Jr. has written several (eight so far) espionage books, all featuring Blackford "Blacky" Oakes, who is a patriot and a Communist hater. All are set solidly in the cold war period of the Eisenhower and Kennedy years, even though the latest was written in 1988 (*Mongoose, R.I.P.*).

What mysteries feature Police Commissioner Theodore Roosevelt?

The Lunatic Fringe (1980), by William L. DeAndrea has Roosevelt as its protagonist and detective. Another recent title is Caleb Carr's *The Alienist* (1994).

Which former First Daughter has a successful mystery series?

Margaret Truman. The first in the series is *Murder in the White House* (1980).

Firsts, Lasts, and Onlies

Have any Nobel Prize winners ever written mysteries?
Yes, they have. The list is longer than you might think and includes Heinrich Böll, Pearl Buck, T. S. Eliot, William Faulkner, Ernest Hemingway, John Galsworthy, Rudyard Kipling, Sinclair Lewis, Bertrand Russell, George Bernard Shaw, and John Steinbeck. Some wrote full-length mysteries and all had stories published in *Ellery Queen's Mystery Magazine*.

In what mystery does the heiress to a fabulous perfume formula get eaten by Cornish slugs?
The Trouble with Product X (1966), by Joan Aiken, who had a peculiarly dark sense of humor.

Which "bad boy" of avant-garde music also wrote mysteries?
George Antheil, who was quite a figure in the music world of the 1920s—his *Ballet Mécanique* was much admired by Ezra Pound and featured sixteen pianos, some buzzers, an airplane propeller and an electric drill—wrote two mystery stories under the pseudo-

nym Stacey Bishop. His story "Death in the Dark" (1930) has an investigator who talks like Ezra Pound and acts like Philo Vance.

What mystery author wrote only one book but can also be credited with getting Myrna Williams to change her name to Myrna Loy?
Paul Cain, whose lone book, *Fast One* (1933), was a big hit with fans, although it was blasted as well as applauded by the critics. Cain wrote a few short stories, but mostly drifted in and out of Hollywood—and that's where he met Myrna Williams. At the time, he was a production assistant and she was a chorus girl.

What is the name of the mystery in which a one-legged journalist-detective searches for a murderer who paints clown faces on the bodies of his victims?
The Black Glass City (1964), by Judson Philips.

Who is the one-armed detective who works out of Greenwich Village?
That would be Michael Collins's character Dan Fortune (né Fortunowski). Losing his arm in his youth while looting a docked ship, he becomes known as "Danny the Pirate." He subsequently gives up crime, travels the world as a merchant seaman, and opens a detective agency. Fortune makes his debut in *Act of Fear* (1967).

In what mystery does an eleven-foot, four-inch woman make an appearance?
The Wailing Frail (1956), by Richard Prather: "She had a seventy-eight-inch bust, forty-six-inch waist, and seventy-two-inch hips-measurements that were exactly right, I thought, for her height of eleven feet, four inches."

In what miserable attempt at a mystery does a fictional Dashiell Hammett try to get a fictional Raymond Chandler to

change the name of his detective?
We hate to even mention this one because someone might waste
time reading it, but it is *Chandler* (1977), by William Denbow. In
it, Hammett tells Chandler: "Let's give the mick a limey name for a
change. . . . More class. I always liked Christopher Marlowe because he was some kind of secret agent. This isn't gumshoe exactly
but it'll do." When Chandler protests, saying that he thinks Chris
is "too pansy," Hammett says, "I had a hound dog once, back in
Maryland when I was a kid. We called him Phil. Phil was a good
old dog, one hell of a good *ole* dog. Why don't we call your
gumshoe *Philip Marlowe*." The rest of the book is no better.

Do any mysteries take place at a nudist colony?
John Ball's *The Cool Cottontail* (1966) is an involved but credible
mystery set in a nudist resort in the mountains of Southern California.

**What sleuth earns money to pay for his detective correspon-
dence course by working as a grocery delivery boy?**
Paul W. Fairman created the character Wally Watts, who at eigh-
teen years old is one of the youngest detectives in adult fiction.
Fairman's stories are composed of letters back and forth between
Watts and the Watchful Eye Detective School of New York City. See
"Wally, the Watchful Eye" (1960).

**What seventy-year-old crime solver is an excellent house-
keeper who lives in a trailer, is a great cook, and mixes a mean
martini?**
Erle Stanley Gardner's Gramps Wiggin, who has no fixed address
and occasionally smuggles booze and sugar into the country from
Mexico. See *The Case of the Smoking Chimney* (1943).

What is the name of the dwarf detective?
Dr. Robert Frederickson, "Mongo," the creation of George C. Chesbro. He is an ex–circus acrobat, who gives up performing to be-

come a professor of criminology, which he also gives up to sleuth full-time. The first "Mongo" book is *Shadow of a Broken Man* (1977).

What is the name of the baseball mystery that has a former minor-leaguer as the detective? I think Mickey Mantle makes a cameo appearance.

Mantle does indeed show up, and the book is *Five O'Clock Lightning* (1982), by William L. DeAndrea. It is set in 1953, and Russ Garrett is the detective and former ballplayer who solves the murder of a red-baiting congressman.

In what mystery, set on the Upper West Side of Manhattan, is the absence of cockroaches a clue?

Unorthodox Practices (1989), by Marissa Piesman. Nina Fischman, a Housing Court attorney, and her mother, Ida, are on the case when two reasonably healthy elderly tenants on West End Avenue die suddenly, opening up two prime leases any New Yorker might kill for. Any New Yorker would also know something is fishy when it's discovered that neither apartment had cockroaches.

Has there ever been a blind detective?

Yes, there are several, but one of the best is one Max Carrados, created by Ernest Bramah Smith. The blind detective appears in *Max Carrados* (1914), *The Eyes of Max Carrados* (1923), and *Max Carrados' Mysteries* (1927). Carrados may be blind but he is served well by an ultradeveloped auditory nerve that enables him to hear sounds inaudible to others. He also knows when a man is wearing a false mustache because he carries "a five-yard aura of spirit gum, emphasized by a warm perspiring skin."

Have any of the blind detectives developed a talent for shooting at sounds?

Baynard Kendrick's Captain Duncan Maclain was blinded in World War I and like most blind detectives honed his other senses to make up for his loss. He was aided by his trusty dogs, Schnuke and Dreist. The first book in the series is *The Odor of Violets* (1941).

In what mystery must the detective investigate the murder of his own father, who has been found dead, wearing spangled tights and strapped into a medieval torture machine?
This happens in Robert Barnard's *Sheer Torture* (1981), which features Perry Trethowan, a Scotland Yard detective.

What detective is an ex-con and an urban vigilante who has no phone, no papers, and pays no rent?
That would be Andrew Vachss's character Burke, who is unique in that he is neither an ex-cop nor a lone knight, but an ex-con with born-again ideals. Burke first appears in *Flood* (1985).

Who was the first author to write of fingerprinting as a means of identification?
None other than Mark Twain, who first developed the idea in a short story in 1883, and expanded on it in *The Tragedy of Pudd'nhead Wilson* (1894) where, in order to explain a crime, Pudd'nhead demonstrates how everyone's fingerprints are different. Twain wrote several other detective stories including "A Double-Barrelled Detective Story" (1902) and "Tom Sawyer, Detective" (1896).

Which detective story features the first appearance of a lie detector?
"The Man Higher Up," by Edwin Balmer and William B. Macharg in *Scientific Detective Monthly* (1930).

What detective uses something called *pilpul* to help solve his cases?
Harry Kemelman's detective, Rabbi David Small, uses *pilpul*, a form of Jewish reasoning, to help crack his cases. Small first appears in *Friday the Rabbi Slept Late* (1964).

The Subject Is Murder

It seems that amnesia turns up quite a bit in mysteries. Just how many mysteries use this gimmick and do any of them stand out in terms of quality?

Amnesia turns up so often that it's rather difficult to find an accurate number, but at after a quick count we come up with sixty-six, three of them by L. P. Davies (*Who Is Lewis Pinder,* 1966; *Give Me Back Myself,* 1971; *What Did I Do Tomorrow?* 1973). One of the best and certainly the most famous is Francis Beeding's *The House of Dr. Edwardes* (1928), which Alfred Hitchcock made into the movie *Spellbound.* Other authors of quality who worked in the amnesia field include: Margery Allingham (*Traitor's Purse,* 1941); Eric Ambler (*The Dark Frontier,* 1936); Fredric Brown (*We All Killed Grandma,* 1952); Robert Ludlum (*The Bourne Identity,* 1980); Rex Stout (*The Black Mountain,* 1954); and Cornell Woolrich (*The Black Curtain,* 1941). A fine recent example is Anne Perry's *The Face of a Stranger* (1991), featuring Inspector Monk.

Have there been any mysteries set on trains other than Agatha

Christie's *Murder on the Orient Express* (1934) and Dick Francis's *The Edge* (1988)?

Sure. Here are some in reverse chronological order:

1987	*Murder on the Long Straight,* by Charlotte Yarborough
1985	*Corpse Cargo,* by Grant Stockbridge
1984	*The Golden Express,* by Derek Lambert
1982	*Maxwell's Train,* by Christopher Hyde
1977	*Trans-Siberian Express,* by Warren Adler
1977	*Avalanche Express,* by Colin Forbes
1974	*Breakheart Pass,* by Alistair MacLean
1964	*Butcher of Belgrade,* by Nick Carter
1963	*10:30 from Marseilles,* by Sebastian Japrisot
1950	*Strangers on a Train,* by Patricia Highsmith
1934	*Obelists on Route,* by Charles Daly King
1932	*Stamboul Express,* by Graham Greene

This is by no means a complete list, but it should get you started.

Besides Agatha Christie's Miss Marple, have there been any geriatric sleuths?
Yes, and even a geriatric hit woman, Evelyn Smith's Miss Melville. Other elderly detectives include Paul Gallico's Miss Arris; Anthony Mancini's Minnie Santangelo; Heron Carvic's Miss Seeton; Patricia Wentworth's Miss Silver; Dorothy Gilman's Mrs. Pollifax; Stuart Palmer's Hildegarde Withers; and Charles Goldstein's Max Gutman.

Which Fredric Brown novel takes place at a carnival?
Madball (1953).

Besides Dorothy L. Sayers's *Murder Must Advertise* (1933) are any other mysteries set in the advertising world?
The high-pressure, high-powered world of advertising has attracted many mystery writers, where it seems they find a perfect setting for envy, jealousy, and murder. Rex Stout set two Nero Wolfe books in the ad world, *And Be a Villain* (1948) and *Before Midnight* (1955), as did Julian Symons, who wrote *The 31st of Feb-*

ruary (1951) and *A Man Called Jones* (1947). Others worth noting include *Plain Murder* (1930), by C. S. Forester, *Murder à la Mode* (1963), by Patricia Moyes, and *Death of an Adman* (1954), by Alfred Eichler.

Why are so many mysteries set on ocean liners?
Ocean liners were glamorous, romantic, and, most important, self-contained units—small worlds where a murder could have a huge impact. Try C. P. Snow's *Death Under Sail* (1932), or Ngaio Marsh's *Singing in the Shrouds* (1958).

What mystery series is set in a department store?
There are actually several, all written when department stores were a bit more glamorous than they are today. The most memorable of these is the one by Spencer Dean, featuring Don Cadee, the director of security at "Ambletts." The first in the series is *Murder on Delivery* (1957).

Are there any mysteries with an archaeological theme?
Archaeology (including Egyptology and anthropology) is one of the more popular mystery subjects, with well over one hundred titles devoted to it. These mysteries generally involve exotic locales, buried treasures, occasional curses, and a sense of history. A long-forgotten crime is often unburied. Elizabeth Peters's mysteries feature amateur Egyptologist Amelia Peabody (*Crocodile on the Sandbank*, 1975). Agatha Christie was married to a famous archaeologist, Sir Max Mallowan, and wrote three mysteries of this type: *Death Comes as the End* (1944), *Murder in Mesopotamia* (1936), and *They Came to Baghdad* (1951). Some other archaeological mysteries of note: R. Austin Freeman's *The Eye of Osiris* (1912), Carter Dickson's *The Curse of the Bronze Lamp* (1945), and Nicholas Blake's *The Widow's Cruise* (1959).

What mysteries are set in the milieu of the art world?
The world of painting and sculpture has attracted hundreds of

mystery authors. The murder often takes place in a great museum, or maybe the artist is found dead in his or her studio. The most famous art mystery is perhaps Dorothy L. Sayers's *Five Red Herrings* (1931), and Michael Innes has written several excellent art mysteries: *Silence Obsessed* (1961), *A Family Affair* (1966), and *The Mysterious Commission* (1975). Oliver Banks, who has a Ph.D. in art history, has written two vivid and authentic art mysteries: *The Rembrandt Panel* (1980) and *The Caravaggio Obsession* (1984).

Are any mysteries set during a "mystery weekend?"

At least two: *Murder on a Mystery Tour* (1987), by Marion Babson, and *Murder at the Murder at the Mimosa Inn* (1986), by Joan Hess.

What series features that middle-aged gardener Celia Grant?

John Sherwood writes about amateur detective Celia Grant, a widowed horticulturist. The first book in the series is *Green Trigger Fingers* (1984).

Who are some other detectives who enjoy gardening?

Here are a few: Sergeant Cuff, Senator Wentworth, Nero Wolfe, Father Bredder, Webster Flagg, and Jane Marple.

What recent mystery is set in the world of rare book dealers and collectors?

Booked to Die (1992), by John Dunning, features Cliff Janeway, a former Denver homicide detective who becomes a dealer in rare books. It is an interesting look into a strange and quirky profession, and by the way, *Booked to Die* itself has become collectible. A first edition is currently worth about $150. Elizabeth Daly's detective Henry Gamadge (*Unexpected Night*, 1940), is a bibliophile and works as a consultant on old books and manuscripts.

Are there any mysteries set during Christmas?

There are several: Agatha Christie's *Murder for Christmas* (1939);

Michael Innes's *Christmas at Candleshoe* (1953); Ed McBain's *Sadie When She Died* (1972); James McClure's *Gooseberry Fool* (1974); and many merry more.

Are there any baseball mysteries?

Does the infield fly rule qualify? How about Robert Parker's *Mortal Stakes* (1975), Paul Benjamin's *Squeeze Play* (1983), L. L. Enger's *Comeback* (1990), and Richard Rosen's Edgar Award–winning *Strike Three, You're Dead* (1984).

Exotic Locales

What detective, as an infant, was found next to his dead mother under a tree? Hint: Shortly after this event, the child was named by a matron who observed him trying to eat a biography of a late French emperor.

Despite his tragic beginning, Arthur W. Upfield's Australian-based detective Napoleon Bonaparte (Bony to his friends) later grew into quite a detective, making his first appearance in *The Barrakee Mystery* (1929).

What South African mystery series features an Afrikaner lieutenant and a Zulu sergeant?

Lieutenant Tromp Kramer and Sergeant Zondi are characters in James McClure's series, starting with *Steam Pig* (1971).

Any mysteries set in Afghanistan?

Here Comes a Hero (1968), by Lawrence Block. It features Evan Tanner, an agent with permanent insomnia.

What mystery is set in a Franciscan abbey in the fourteenth century?
Umberto Eco's avant-garde crime novel *Name of the Rose* (1980, published in English in 1983). The detective, William of Baskerville, owes much to Conan Doyle in appearance and manner as well as in name.

What is the name of a spy novel set in the Sudan?
Charles McCarry's *Miernik Dossier* (1973), featuring Paul Christopher.

What long-running mystery series takes place in India?
H. R. F. Keating's Inspector Ghote (pronounced Go-tay) series started in 1965 with *The Perfect Murder* and currently stands at fifteen titles, the most recent being *The Iciest Sin* (1990). While Keating's books provide a reasonably accurate picture of today's India, he admits that for the first ten years of the series he had never visited the country.

What series takes place in Amsterdam?
The Inspector Piet Van der Valk series, by Nicolas Freeling. The first in the series is *Love in Amsterdam* (1962).

What Victorian police procedural series uses actual nineteenth-century events such as an endurance race, bare-fist boxing, and Irish dynamiters?
Peter Lovesey's series featuring the stolidly intelligent Sergeant Cribb and his pompous superior Inspector Jowet. The books on the subjects mentioned above are, in order: *Wobble to Death* (1970), *The Detective Wore Silk Drawers* (1971), and *Tick of Death* (1974).

Has Athens been the setting for a mystery?
Yes, in Patricia Highsmith's *Two Faces of January* (1964).

Who is the Swedish couple who write mysteries?
Together, Per Wahlöö and Maj Sjöwall wrote ten mysteries, all featuring the laconic and competent Swedish detective Martin Beck. Wahlöö and Sjöwall each wrote alternate chapters after doing much careful research and detailed synopses. Their aim was to "use the crime novel as a scalpel cutting open the belly of an ideologically pauperized and morally debatable so-called welfare state of the bourgeois type." (Perhaps it loses something in the translation.) The pair's main contribution to the genre was their ability to use a popular form to put forward complex theories. The first book in the series is *Roseanna* (1967).

In which rare case does the corpulent and sedentary detective Nero Wolfe leave not only his house but the country?
Rex Stout's Character Nero Wolfe and his assistant, Archie Goodwin, fly to Montenegro to solve a case in *The Black Mountain* (1954).

What author of suspense novels has written several books set in Austria?
Helen MacInnes in *The Salzburg Connection* (1968) and *Above Suspicion* (1941).

Can you name the flamboyant liaison officer between the Brazilian police and Interpol who is partial to Reserva San Juan cognac and U.S. cigarettes?
Captain Jose Da Silva—Zé to his friends—was created by Robert L. Fish, who won an Edgar Award for *The Fugitive* in 1962.

What's the name of the hard-boiled detective who walks down the mean streets of Sydney, Australia?
With the character of Cliff Hardy, Peter Corris has created an Aussie version of Travis McGee meets Lew Archer. Invariably dressed in a leather jacket and jeans, Hardy is smart, tough, and determined. The first in the series is *The Dying Trade* (1982).

Are there any mysteries set in Baghdad?
A few. Probably the best-known is *They Came to Baghdad* (1951), by Agatha Christie.

What mystery begins in People's Park in Berkeley, California?
As a Favor (1984), by Susan Dunlap, which stars homicide detective Jill Smith.

Has a mystery ever been set in the Bahamas?
John D. MacDonald's *Man of Affairs* (1957).

How about the former Belgian Congo?
Take a look at Victor Canning's *Black Flamingo* (1962) or Graham Greene's *A Burnt-out Case* (1961).

Are there any mysteries set in the Caribbean?
Try Agatha Christie's *Caribbean Mystery* (1964) or Patricia Moyes's *To Kill a Coconut* (1977).

Name a suspense novel set in Borneo.
Gavin Black's *You Want to Die, Johnny?* (1966).

Are there any mysteries set in Budapest?
The excellent book *The Man Who Went Up in Smoke* (1969) by Per Wahlöö and Maj Sjöwall.

What writer of thrillers was formerly a Swiss banker?
Paul Erdman, who after serving a term in prison for juggling some figures went on to write thrillers, including *The Billion Dollar Sure Thing* (1973).

Can you name any mysteries set in Zambia?
For something light and fun, try *Mrs. Pollifax on Safari* (1977), by Dorothy Gilman.

What's the best crime novel you can think of set in Vienna?
That's easy. Graham Greene's *The Third Man* (1950).

What is the name of the Dick Francis novel set in Norway?
Slay-Ride (1973), an excellent book about Norwegian racing as well as an insightful novel about parenting.

What is the name of the Patricia Highsmith novel set in Mexico City?
A Game for the Living (1958). For another good mystery set in Mexico City, take a look at *An Easy Thing* (1990), by Paco Ignacio Taibo II.

Are there any good mysteries set in Hong Kong?
Try Jonathan Gash's *Jade Woman* (1988), which features Lovejoy, the sometimes unscrupulous antique dealer and sleuth. Or for espionage see John le Carré's *Honourable Schoolboy* (1977). William Marshall's Yellowthread Street series is a police procedural set in Hong Kong. The first in the series is *The Yellowthread Street* (1975).

What mystery series takes place in Ancient Rome?
There are currently two very good ones. One by Lindsey Davis (*Silver Pigs*, 1989) and another by John Maddox Roberts (*SPQR*, 1990).

Are there any mysteries set in Turkey?
Nothing Is the Number When You Die (1965), by Joan Fleming.

Which famous British mystery writer was born in Singapore?
Leslie Charteris, the creator of the Saint, was born in Singapore on
May 12, 1907.

Murderous Miscellanea

Is *Crime and Punishment* a mystery?
While there is most definitely a murder and some investigation work, *Crime and Punishment,* by Fyodor Dostoevsky (1866), is first and foremost concerned with the human condition, not with the process of detection. This makes it a novel, not a mystery.

Why is it that some mysteries have one title in the United States and another in the United Kingdom, like Agatha Christie's *Why Didn't They Ask Evans?* which became *The Boomerang Clue?*
Sometimes there is a legitimate reason, such as a word in the title that might have a slightly different meaning in one country than it does in the other. But usually it's merely the whim of the publisher. Here are some other switches they pulled on Christie: *The Sittaford Mystery* became *The Murder at Hazelmoor,* while *Lord Edgware Dies* became *Thirteen at Dinner. Murder on the Orient Express* became *Murder in the Calais Coach*—and was subsequently changed back after the success of the movie.

Where in New York did Nero Wolfe live?
Rex Stout's character Nero Wolfe lived in a three-story brownstone on the north side of West 35th Street, though if you are energetic enough to check you'll find there are no brownstones on West 35th Street. According to the Wolfe Pack, an organization of Nero Wolfe fans, this address is a mysterious deception, and Wolfe actually lived on West 22nd Street, a street with plenty of brownstones.

Did the literary critic Edmund Wilson write an essay damning all detective fiction as garbage?
In 1959 Wilson wrote in *The New Yorker* that "with so many fine books to be read . . . there is no need to bore ourselves with this rubbish." Edmund's essay, entitled "Who Cares Who Killed Roger Ackroyd?" reportedly did much to damage the reputation and sales figures of the whole mystery genre.

Didn't the author of *Winnie the Pooh* write a mystery?
Yes. A. A. Milne wrote *The Red House Mystery* in 1922. The book is typical of the cozy school—light and amusing, with an easy way with murder—which was popular at the time. Milne also wrote one other mystery, *Four Days' Wonder* (1933).

In which mystery does T. S. Eliot appear on the very first page?
In Nicholas Blake's first book, *A Question of Proof* (1935). Blake brought to the mystery a distinct literary tone, and in his early books a left-wing political attitude.

Which mystery author wrote a series with the word "puzzle" in most of his titles?
Patrick Quentin—who is actually two authors, Hugh Wheeler and Richard Wilson Webb—wrote a series that lasted from 1936 to 1948, featuring Peter Duluth, a former Broadway producer. All the titles begin with *Puzzle for,* including: . . . *Fools,* . . . *Players,* . . . *Puppets,* . . . *Wantons,* . . . *Friends,* and . . . *Pilgrims.*

In what mystery is the victim murdered on an operating table under the eyes of seven witnesses?
Christianna Brand's *Green for Danger* (1944), which is set in a military hospital during World War II.

What is the Edgar Award?
The Edgar Allan Poe Awards are given once a year by an association called Mystery Writers of America. The Edgar is the Oscar of the mystery world and there are three main categories: Best Novel, Best First Novel by an American, and Best Paperback Original. The first Edgar was awarded to Thomas Walsh in 1951 for *Nightmare in Manhattan.*

Where did the term "red herring" come from?
A red herring is a false clue meant to distract from the real culprit, and the term has its origins in seventeenth-century England. It seems that certain troublemakers with an acute sense of mischief would buy herrings and smoke them, thereby giving them a reddish color, and then drag them through the woods just before a fox hunt. The fishy scent would confuse the hounds, allowing the fox to escape. Ever since, red herrings have been synonymous with attempts to deceive.

Is there a rabbi detective?
Harry Kemelman's detective, Rabbi David Small, is too honest and too absent-minded for his own good. You can recognize a Rabbi Small book because most of them have a day of the week in the title, like *Friday the Rabbi Slept Late* (1964).

In what mystery is a pair of slippers embroidered with Chinese characters a major and recurring clue?
Earl Derr Biggers's *Behind That Curtain* (1928). One foggy January night in London a man is found dead in his private office; his shoes are on his desk and he is wearing the aforementioned Chinese slip-

pers. Charlie Chan is summoned to the case when another man is found murdered—also wearing Chinese slippers.

What fictional detective did Ellery Queen once describe as "a Sherlock Holmes and an Arsène Lupin crammed simultaneously into the same pair of pants?"
That would be Philip MacDonald's detective Dr. Alcazar, whose face is of "extraordinary pallor: his dark eyes, large and lustrous and glowing. His black, well-tended hair, impressively gray at the temples, surmounted an Olympian brow. . . ." He's one of the few clairvoyant/detectives.

Speaking of Philip MacDonald, can you name Dr. Alcazar's weight-guesser friend?
The ever loyal Avvie du Pois.

It seems there are several very heavy detectives. Can you give us some exact weights?

Nero Wolfe:	Nearly 300 lbs.
Chief Inspector Dover:	240 lbs.
Gideon Fell:	250 lbs.
Bertha Cool:	200 lbs.

Other "large" detectives include: George Smiley, Charlie Chan, Father Brown, Martin Hewitt, Inspector Hanaud, Sergeant Beef, and Inspector Bucket.

What part-time detective is the editor of *The Broadway Times* and lives above a Times Square flea circus?
David Alexander's Bart Hardin, who's also a former Marine and Korean War hero. See *Die, Little Goose* (1956).

What is the name of Lord Peter Wimsey's man Friday?

His name is Bunter and he served as sergeant under Captain Wimsey in France. Bunter is a bibliophile and expert photographer who also brews a perfect cup of coffee.

What famous crime novel author wrote a lesbian coming-of-age novel in the 1950s?
Patricia Highsmith wrote *The Price of Salt* (1952) under the pseudonym Claire Morgan. It is a wonderfully bittersweet novel that has been largely ignored in the United States but highly acclaimed in Europe, where its title is *Carol.*

Are there any mysteries featuring a homosexual detective?
One of the first openly gay detectives is George Baxt's Pharoah Love, who first appears in *A Queer Kind of Death* (1966). The most successful series of this type is Joseph Hansen's featuring Dave Brandstetter, a gay insurance investigator who works in Los Angeles. The first in the twelve-book series is *Fadeout* (1979) and the latest is *A Country of Old Men* (1991).

Are there any lesbian detectives?
Katherine Forrest writes about a Los Angeles Police Department homicide detective named Kate Delafield who appears in *Amateur City* (1987), *Murder at the Nightwood Bar* (1987), and *Beverly Malibu* (1990). Barbara Wilson's character Pam Nilsen, the part-owner of a left-wing printing press, can be found in *Murder in the Collective* (1984), *Sisters of the Road* (1986), and *The Dog Collar Murders* (1989). Two other fine writers of lesbian detective series are Ellen Hart (*Hallowed Murder,* 1989) and Sandra Scoppettone (*Everything You Have Is Mine,* 1992).

What mystery is just packed with the poetry of W. H. Auden?
Poetic Justice (1970), by Amanda Cross, who is really retired Columbia University professor Carolyn Heilbrun. Her detective is Professor Kate Fansler.

Has a publisher's error ever been responsible for changing the outcome of a mystery?
In 1946 the publisher Charles Scribner's Sons accidentally left off the final chapter of Margerie Bonner's *The Last Twist of the Knife*, which was later found in the bottom drawer of the editor's desk. The publisher tried to make amends by producing the final chapter in a special pamphlet offered at no cost to any reader who was unsatisfied. According to Charles Scribner Jr., no requests for the pamphlet were ever received.

What was the favorite drink of Dashiell Hammett's characters Nick and Nora Charles?
They drank martinis mixed as follows: 3 ounces of gin; 1 ounce of vermouth. Nick and Nora appeared in several movies but in only one book, *The Thin Man* (1934).

What does Georges Simenon's character Jules Maigret call his wife?
Her name is Louise, but he calls her "Madame Maigret." She calls him simply "Maigret."

What is the name of the character who is the company detective for a television network?
Matt Cobb, who first appeared in *Killed in the Ratings* (1978), by William L. DeAndrea. The book won that year's Edgar Allan Poe Award for best first mystery.

What British mystery author once described a character's nose as "less accipitrine than columbaceous"?
That was Peter Dickinson, who usually writes with much flair and intelligence—but like most good writers he sometimes trips up. Try *The Poison Oracle* (1974).

What is the name of that sophisticated, suburban, crime-solving couple who appeared in the 1940s?
Mr. and Mrs. North. They were created by the husband and wife team of Frances and Richard Lockridge in 1940 (*The Norths Meet Murder*). The Norths star in over two dozen books throughout the 1950s and ending in 1963.

What are the Norths' first names?
Pam and Jerry.

How about the name of the Norths' cat?
Pam and Jerry occasionally did some investigating, but they never missed a cocktail hour. Their cat is named Martini.

Who is the author of such wacky titles as *Oh! Where Are Bloody Mary's Earrings?* (1972), *Let's Talk of Graves, of Worms, and Epitaphs* (1975), and *The Month of the Mangled Models* (1977)?
Robert Player is the British mystery author with the strange titles, though the books themselves are fairly traditional.

What mystery takes its title from the text of Brahms's Four Serious Songs?
The Beast Must Die (1938), by Nicholas Blake. The Brahms text is a paraphrase from the Book of Ecclesiastes, "The beast must die, the man dieth also, yea both must die."

In what grim crime novel does the protagonist let a parolee go free who was hired to kill him, quit hunting for the man who raped his sister, and go back to live with the woman who hired the parolee?
David Goodis's *The Moon in the Gutter* (1953). Goodis's books are so dark and devoid of hope that there is little suspense. They are not so much mysteries as bitter slices of life.

I know Sherlock Holmes played the violin and Nero Wolfe grew orchids, but what are some other detectives' hobbies?
Hildegarde Withers raises tropical fish; Sergeant Beef plays darts; Charlie Chan likes swimming and chess; J. G. Reader plays patience; Ellery Queen collects rare books; and Captain Duncan Maclain, who is blind, assembles jigsaw puzzles.

What suspense novel begins and ends with a class of boys reading from Shakespeare's *A Midsummer Night's Dream*?
The Paper Dolls (1964), by L. P. Davies. Two young schoolteachers uncover supernatural phenomena at the school and fall in love.

In Frederick Knott's 1966 Broadway play *Wait Until Dark,* Lee Remick won a Tony Award as a blind woman terrorized by a psychopath (Alan Arkin). What unusual—and illegal—thing did the producers get permission to do at every performance for the entire run of the play?
Your clue is in the play's title. In the final moments, Remick equalized her chances of survival by turning off all the lights in her house, putting the villain on her level. For approximately three minutes at each performance, every light in the Barrymore Theatre was extinguished—including the emergency exit signs—in direct violation of New York State laws. In the 1967 movie version with Audrey Hepburn, a similar, startling effect was achieved with several moments of dark screen.

Match the "Watson" with his or her creator.
1. Abigail Sanderson   a. Elizabeth George
2. Mike Burden   b. Robert Crais
3. Joe Pike   c. Reginald Hill
4. Barbara Havers   d. Harry Kemelman
5. Dermot Craddock   e. E. X. Giroux
6. Peter Pascoe   f. Agatha Christie
7. Chief Lanigan   g. Ruth Rendell

1.e., 2.g., 3.b., 4.a., 5.f., 6.c., 7.d.

What mystery series is co-written by a cat?
Sneaky Pie Brown is listed as the co-author along with her owner, Rita Mae Brown, for a series that starts with *Wish You Were Here* (1990).

What female sleuth writes a column called "A Dog's Life"?
Holly Winter, Susan Conant's detective. She has a pet malamute and each of the books is set in the world of dog shows, groomers, and trainers. The first book in the series is *Dead and Doggone* (1990).

Where did the term "private eye" come from?
It comes from Allan Pinkerton's detective agency, which was founded in the mid-nineteenth century. The Pinkerton slogan was "We never sleep," and had as its symbol a wide-open eye.

What is the the code of the hard-boiled detective?
It was perhaps best stated by Raymond Chandler: "Down these mean streets a man must go who is not himself mean."

Where does every murder in *The Maltese Falcon* (1930) take place?
Offstage.

What was Jack Webb's badge number on the television show *Dragnet*?
It was 714. He chose it because it was the number of home runs hit by Babe Ruth.

Killer Titles

Who wrote *Abracadaver*?
Peter Lovesey wrote a book by this title in 1972, and Ralph McInerny borrowed the title in 1989. Ken Crossen wrote a book called *Abra-Cadaver* in 1958 under the pseudonym Christopher Monig.

How many mystery titles begin with "All Men Are . . ."?
All Men Are Liars (1948), by Elwin Strange; *All Men Are Lonely Now* (1967), by Francis Clifford; and *All Men Are Murderers* (1958), by Charity Blackstock.

How many mysteries are titled *And Be a Villain*?
Three. One by Rex Stout (1948), one by Laurence Meynell (1939), and one by Joanna Cannan (1958).

Who wrote the mystery *Angel*?
Gil Brewer used this title in 1960, as did Gerald Verner in 1939. Carter Brown added an exclamation point for his 1962 *Angel!* An-

other popular "Angel" title is *Angel of Death,* which has been used by P. D. Ballard (1974), James Anderson (1978), Philip Loraine (1961), and Anthea Cohen (1983).

Who wrote *Animal-Lover's Book of Beastly Murder?*
Patricia Highsmith (1975).

What author came up with the title *Author Bites the Dust?*
Arthur Upfield (1948), who has been cited as a major influence by Tony Hillerman.

Who wrote *Baby in the Icebox?*
James M. Cain (1981).

Who wrote *The Big Fix?*
Evan Hunter did in 1952, Ed Lacy in 1960, and Roger Simon in 1973.

How many mysteries have "bimbo" in the title?
Bimbos of the Death Sun (1989), by Sharon McCrumb and *Bimbo Heaven* (1990), by Marvin Albert.

Who wrote *Black Is the Colour of My True-Love's Heart?*
Ellis Peters (1967).

Isn't there a mystery entitled *Blind Man with a Pistol?*
Yes. It was written by Chester Himes in 1969.

Are there any good mystery titles about blondes?
We prefer to say "women with blond hair," but, yes, there are several. How about *Blonde on a Broomstick* (1966), by Carter Brown, or

Blonde, Beautiful, and—Blam! (1956), also by Brown. Our personal favorite is *Blondie Iscariot* (1948), by Edgar Lustgarten.

Who wrote *Burden of Proof*?
Scott Turow wrote the latest *Burden of Proof* (1990), but there have been at least three others: one by Victor Canning in 1956, one by Jeffrey Ashford in 1962, and another by Mary Challis (pseudonym for Sara Woods) in 1980.

Who is responsible for penning *The Cancelled Czech*?
Lawrence Block wrote it in 1966. It featured Evan Tanner, an agent who had permanent insomnia.

Doesn't Block also have some odd titles about a burglar?
He's written four in the burglar series, all featuring Bernie Rhodenbarr. They are: *Burglars Can't Be Choosers* (1977), *The Burglar Who Liked to Quote Kipling* (1979), *The Burglar Who Studied Spinoza* (1981), and *The Burglar Who Painted Like Mondrian* (1983).

Who came up with the nifty title *Catch a Falling Clown*?
Stuart Kaminsky (1982).

P. D. James wrote *Cover Her Face* (1962), but who wrote *Cover His Face*?
Thomas Kyd (1949).

Isn't there a mystery about gardening called *The Curse of the Giant Hogweed*?
Yes. It was written by Charlotte Macleod in 1985 and features Professor Peter Shandy, co-developer of the Balaclava Buster rutabaga.

Who wrote *Dead Men Don't Ski*?

Patricia Moyes, in 1959. It was her first book.

How many authors have used *Dead Ringer* for a title?
At least four. Fredric Brown wrote the most famous one in 1948. James Hadley Chase (1955), Arthur Lyons (1977), and Roger Ormerod (1985) also used the title.

What author wrote both *Death of a Doxy* and *Death of a Dude*?
Rex Stout in 1966 and 1969, respectively.

Which author wrote *Death in the Fifth Position*?
Edgar Box (pseudonym for Gore Vidal) in 1952.

Who wrote *Death Is for Losers*?
William Nolan in 1968. Nolan's first book was *Nolan's Run* (1967), which was later made into a successful movie and television series, both titled *Logan's Run*.

Who wrote *So Nude, So Dead*?
Ed McBain, writing as Richard Marsten, in 1956. Just to make things more complicated, Ed McBain is a pseudonym for Evan Hunter.

And who wrote *So Rich, So Dead*?
Gil Brewer (1951).

And how about *So Rich, So Lovely, and So Dead*?
Harold Q. Masur (1952).

Who penned *Swing Low, Sweet Harriet*?
George Baxt, in 1967.

And who wrote *Swing Low Swing Dead*?
Frank Gruber in 1964.

Who wrote *The Swell-Looking Babe*?
That's one of our favorite titles (not books, just titles) and it was written by Jim Thompson in 1954.

Who wrote *Where There's a Will*?
Mary Roberts Rinehart (1912), Rex Stout (1940), Ellis Peters (1960), and Sara Woods (1980).

Who wrote *The Wench Is Dead*?
Colin Dexter (1989) and Fredric Brown (1955).

Who wrote *She Came Too Late*?
Mary Wings in 1986. She is also the author of *She Came in a Flash* (1988).

What father of a famous mystery author wrote *The Rat Began to Gnaw the Rope* and *The Rope Began to Hang the Butcher*?
Sue Grafton's father, C. W. Grafton, in 1944 and 1945.

Who wrote *Panic*?
Horace McCloy in 1944. John Creasey wrote *Panic!* in 1939, as did Bill Pronzini in 1972. There have also been *Panic in Box C* (1966), by John Dickson Carr; *Panic in Paradise* (1951), by Alan Amos; *Panic in Philly* (1973), by Don Pendleton; *Panic of '89* (1986), by Paul Erdman; and *Panic Party* (1934), by Anthony Berkeley.

Now a Major Motion Picture

What mystery novel did Alfred Hitchcock draw upon for his movie *Suspicion* (1941)?
Suspicion was based on *Before the Fact* (1932), by Frances Iles, and the film is pretty faithful to the book except for the ending. By the way, Frances Iles is a pseudonym for Anthony Berkeley, who is best known for *The Poisoned Chocolates Case* (1929).

Who played the role of the murderer in the film version of Agatha Christie's *And Then There Were None* (1939)?
That depends. *And Then There Were None* has been made into a major motion picture four times. First came René Clair's classic 1945 version, with Barry Fitzgerald playing the murderer, and then the book was filmed twice more under the title *Ten Little Indians*: Wilfred Hyde-White was the villain in 1966; and in 1975, the part was played by Richard Attenborough. In 1989 it was again filmed as *And Then There Were None* and Donald Pleasence is the murderer in this one, which is set in Africa, with the victims on a safari. This epic also stars Frank Stallone (Sly's brother) as our hero and Brenda Vaccaro as the governess who gets stung.

For extra credit: Who played the role of the murderer in the original Broadway production of *Ten Little Indians* (1944)?
Halliwell Hobbes.

In which movie did Mickey Spillane play his own detective, Mike Hammer?
The Girl Hunters (1963).

Can you name some other big-screen Mike Hammers?
Biff Elliott in *I, The Jury* (1953); Ralph Meeker in *Kiss Me Deadly* (1955); Robert Bray in *My Gun Is Quick* (1957); Armand Assante in *I, The Jury* (1982).

Which Mike Hammer movie was filmed in 3-D?
I, The Jury (1953). It appeared only one year after the book by Mickey Spillane.

In addition to John Barrymore, who played Sherlock Holmes during the silent-film era?
Maurice Costello played Holmes in *The Adventures of Sherlock Holmes* (1903); Harry Benham got the role in *The Sign of the Four* (1913); James Bragington starred in *A Study in Scarlet* (1914); William Gillette was Sherlock Holmes in *Sherlock Holmes* (1916); John Barrymore played the part in *Sherlock Holmes* (1922).

And who played Holmes in the talkies?
Basil Rathbone is the most famous. Others to play the great detective include Clive Brook, Raymond Massey, Nicol Williamson, Robert Stephens, and Christopher Plummer.

Who played Ellery Queen in the 1935 movie *The Spanish Cape Mystery*?
The Spanish Cape Mystery was the first of the Ellery Queen movies,

and the starring role went to Donald Cook. The next to play Ellery was the comic Eddie Quillan; Ralph Bellamy played the detective in later movies, until he was replaced by William Gargan.

Who played the role of Perry Mason in the 1937 movie *The Case of the Stuttering Bishop*?
Donald Woods. William Warren and Ricardo Cortez also played Perry Mason.

In which film series did the star turn over his role to his real-life brother?
The Falcon series originally starred George Sanders, who grew bored with the role and turned it over to his brother, Tom Conway.

What were the final words in the 1941 movie version of *The Maltese Falcon*?
The last word is "Huh?"

In which film does this speech appear? "Big Ed, great big Ed. You know why they call him Big Ed: Because he's got big ideas. Some day he's gonna get a big idea about me—and it's gonna be his last!"
James Cagney delivers this speech in *White Heat* (1949).

Which part did Bette Davis play in the second film version of Dashiell Hammett's *The Maltese Falcon* (1930)?
The film was retitled *Satan Met a Lady* (1936), and the name of Davis's character was also changed, from Brigid O'Shaughnessy to Valerie Purvis.

Didn't the final scene of the movie version of James M. Cain's *Double Indemnity* (1944) get cut?
Yes. The scene was to show Edgar G. Robinson looking through a

window to see Fred MacMurray strapped into the chair in the gas chamber.

Which Charlie Chan film features Boris Karloff as a deranged opera singer?
Charlie Chan at the Opera (1935). With a dubbed voice, Karloff sings Mephistopheles.

How many Thin Man movies were made?
The Thin Man (1934); *After the Thin Man* (1937); *Another Thin Man* (1939); *Shadow of the Thin Man* (1941); *The Thin Man Goes Home* (1941); and *Song of the Thin Man* (1947). That makes six—not bad for a series named after a character ("the thin man") who is the first victim in the first film.

How much money was allocated in the budget for rolling fog in the 1939 movie version of *The Hound of the Baskervilles*?
The sum of $93,000. A vast moor was built on the Fox stages and Holmes's London was painstakingly reproduced. This was the film that was to launch Basil Rathbone as Sherlock Holmes.

What actors have had the chance to play the part of S. S. Van Dine's scholar and dabbler in mystery, Philo Vance?
William Powell was the first, appearing as Vance in *The Canary Murder Case* (1929). Other actors to get the part were: Basil Rathbone, Warren William, Paul Lukas, Edmund Lowe, Grant Richards, and Alan Curtis.

Whom did author Ian Fleming originally want to play the part of Dr. No in the 1962 movie of the same name?
Fleming originally suggested his island neighbor Noel Coward for the role, but Coward declined. Joseph Wiseman did the honors.

What mystery author wrote the play *Rope* (1929), later made into a movie by Alfred Hitchcock?
Patrick Hamilton wrote *Rope,* based on the Nietzschean murder committed by two Chicago teenagers. The film that Hitchcock made in 1948 is usually remembered for a visual gimmick: the entire film appears to be a single, unbroken shot in which the few cuts that do exist are cleverly concealed.

What French novel was Alfred Hitchcock's movie *Vertigo* based on?
Vertigo was based on *D'Entre Les Morts,* by Boileau and Narcejac.

What Hitchcock movie is about a man who was suspected of being Jack the Ripper?
The Lodger (1926), based on the 1913 Marie Belloc Lowndes book of the same title.

Has Poe's "The Murders in the Rue Morgue" ever been filmed?
It was filmed in 1932 with Bela Logosi as a Hoffmannesque Dr. Miracle. There was also a 1954 Warner Bros. version with Karl Malden as Dupin.

Didn't the author of *Solomon's Vineyard* (1941) travel to Hollywood to write for the movies?
Yes. Jonathan Latimer could count among his credits the second film version of Hammett's *The Glass Key* (1942), Kenneth Fearing's *The Big Clock* (1948), and Cornell Woolrich's *The Night Has a Thousand Eyes* (1948).

What mystery film is shot through the eyes of the detective?
Raymond Chandler's *Lady in the Lake* (1947), directed by Robert Montgomery. Philip Marlowe (also played by Montgomery) is seen only when he happens to look in a mirror.

When did Basil Rathbone die?
The screen actor Basil Rathbone, the best-known portrayer of Sherlock Holmes, died on July 21, 1967.

What is the name of the Ethel Lina White novel on which Alfred Hitchcock based his movie *The Lady Vanishes*?
The Wheel Spins (1936), which tells the tale of a young woman on a train discovering that an elderly woman passenger has disappeared. The title refers to the role chance plays in all our lives.

Wasn't *The Bride Wore Black* made into a movie?
Yes it was, by François Truffaut in 1968.

For which of the following films did Alfred Hitchcock receive the Academy Award for Best Director: *Strangers on a Train*, *North By Northwest*, *Vertigo*, *Rebecca*, *Rear Window*, or *Psycho*?
None of the above. Believe it or not, Hitchcock never won the award.

In which mystery film does Vanessa Redgrave say, "What a funny little man!" and Sean Connery reply, "Obviously a Frog"?
This insult was aimed at Hercule Poirot (Albert Finney), who was Belgian, not French, in *Murder on the Orient Express* (1974).

Wasn't there a Nero Wolfe television show in the 1980s?
There was, starring William Conrad as Wolfe, but it only lasted half a season.

What is the British version of *Dragnet*?
Z Cars, which was set in Liverpool and ran from 1960 to 1978.

In what movie does a character named Cody Jarret stand on top of a burning building and shout, "Top of the world, Ma"?
White Heat (1949), directed by Raoul Walsh. Cody Jarret was played by James Cagney.

What great film thriller inspired a real-life jewel heist?
After seeing *Topkapi* (1964), a film based on Eric Ambler's *The Light of Day* (1962), Jack Murphy (aka Murf the Surf) stole the world's largest star sapphire, the Star of India, from New York's Museum of Natural History.

What famous novelist wrote dialogue for the screenplay version of Raymond Chandler's *The Big Sleep* (1939)?
The Big Sleep was made into a movie in 1946. William Faulkner wrote much of the dialogue. Supposedly he had a question about the complex plot and called Chandler for clarification. The story goes that neither of them were able to figure it out and just worked around it.

How did Alfred Hitchcock respond when his collaborator and screenwriter for *Rear Window* (1954) told him that he had won an Edgar Allan Poe Award for scripting the film?
According to the screenwriter himself, John Michael Hayes, Hitchcock said, "You know, they make toilet bowls out of the same thing."

Mystery Writers of America Edgar Allan Poe Awards

BEST NOVEL

1993	*The Sculptress,* by Minette Walters
1992	*Bootlegger's Daughter,* by Margaret Maron
1991	*A Dance at the Slaughterhouse,* by Lawrence Block
1990	*New Orleans Mourning,* by Julie Smith
1989	*Black Cherry Blues,* by James Lee Burke
1988	*A Cold Red Sunrise,* by Stuart M. Kaminsky
1987	*Old Bones,* by Aaron Elkins
1986	*A Dark-Adapted Eye,* by Barbara Vine
1985	*The Suspect,* by L. R. Wright
1984	*Briarpatch,* by Ross Thomas
1983	*La Brava,* by Elmore Leonard
1982	*Billingsgate Shoal,* by Rick Boyer
1981	*Peregrine,* by William Bayer
1980	*Whip Hand,* by Dick Francis
1979	*The Rheingold Route,* by Arthur Maling
1980	*The Eye of the Needle,* by Ken Follett
1977	*Catch Me Kill Me,* by William Hallahan
1976	*Promised Land,* by Robert B. Parker
1975	*Hopscotch,* by Brian Garfield

1974   *Peter's Pence,* by Jon Cleary
1973   *Dance Hall of the Dead,* by Tony Hillerman
1972   *The Lingala Code,* by Warren Kiefer
1971   *The Day of the Jackal,* by Frederick Forsyth
1970   *The Laughing Policeman,* by Maj Sjöwall and Per Wahlöö
1969   *Forfeit,* by Dick Francis
1968   *A Case of Need,* by Jeffrey Hudson
1967   *God Save the Mark,* by Donald E. Westlake
1966   *King of the Rainy Country,* by Nicolas Freeling
1965   *The Quiller Memorandum,* by Adam Hall
1964   *The Spy Who Came in from the Cold,* by John le Carré
1963   *The Light of Day,* by Eric Ambler
1962   *Death and the Joyful Woman,* by Ellis Peters
1961   *Gideon's Fire,* by J. J. Marric
1960   *The Progress of a Crime,* by Julian Symons
1959   *The Hours Before Dawn,* by Celia Fremlin
1958   *The Eighth Circle,* by Stanley Ellin
1957   *Room to Swing,* by Ed Lacy
1956   *A Dram of Poison,* by Charlotte Armstrong
1955   *Beast in View,* by Margaret Millar
1954   *The Long Goodbye,* by Raymond Chandler
1953   *Beat Not the Bones,* by Charlotte Jay

BEST FIRST NOVEL

1993   *A Grave Talent,* by Laurie King
1992   *The Black Echo,* by Michael Connelly
1991   *Slow Motion Riot,* by Peter Blauner
1990   *Post Mortem,* by Patricia Daniels Cornwell
1989   *The Last Billable Hour,* by Susan Wolfe
1988   *Carolina Skeletons,* by David Stout
1987   *Death Among Strangers,* by Deirdre Laiken
1986   *No One Rides for Free,* by Larry Beinhart
1985   *When the Bough Breaks,* by Jonathan Kellerman
1984   *Strike Three, You're Dead,* by Richard Rosen
1983   *The Bay Psalm Book Murder,* by Will Harriss
1982   *The Butcher's Boy,* by Thomas Perry
1981   *Chiefs,* by Stuart Woods
1980   *The Watcher,* by Kay Nolte Smith

1979	*The Lasko Tangent,* by Richard North Patterson
1978	*Killed in the Ratings,* by William L. DeAndrea
1977	*A French Finish,* by Robert Ross
1976	*The Thomas Berryman Number,* by James Patterson
1975	*The Alvarez Journal,* by Rex Burns
1974	*Fletch,* by Gregory McDonald
1973	*The Billion Dollar Sure Thing,* by Paul E. Erdman
1971	*Finding Maubee,* by A. H. Carr
1970	*The Anderson Tapes,* by Lawrence Sanders
1969	*A Time of Predators,* by Joe Gores
1968	Dual Winner:
	Silver Street, by E. Richard Johnson
	The Bait, by Dorothy Uhnak
1967	*Act of Fear,* by Michael Collins
1966	*The Cold War Swap,* by Ross Thomas
1965	*In the Heat of the Night,* by John Ball
1964	*Friday the Rabbi Slept Late,* by Harry Kemelman
1963	*The Florentine Finish,* by Cornelius Hirschberg
1962	*The Fugitive,* by Robert L. Fish
1961	*The Green Stone,* by Suzanne Blanc
1960	*The Man in the Cage,* by John Holbrook Vance
1959	*The Grey Flannel Shroud,* by Henry Slesar
1958	*The Bright Road to Fear,* by Richard Martin Stern
1957	*Knock and Wait a While,* by William Rawle Weeks
1956	*Rebecca's Pride,* by Donald McNutt
1955	*The Perfectionist,* by Lane Kauffman
1954	*Go, Lovely Rose,* by Jean Potts
1953	*A Kiss Before Dying,* by Ira Levin
1952	*Don't Cry for Me,* by William Campbell Gault
1951	*Strangle Hold,* by Mary McMullen
1950	*Nightmare in Manhattan,* by Thomas Walsh
1949	*What a Body!,* by Alan Green
1948	*The Room Upstairs,* by Mildred Davis
1947	*The Fabulous Clipjoint,* by Fredric Brown
1946	*The Horizontal Man,* by Helen Eustis
1945	*Watchful at Night,* by Julius Fast

BEST PAPERBACK ORIGINAL
1993   *Dead Folks' Blues*, by Steven Womack
1992   *A Cold Day for Murder*, by Dana Stabenow
1991   *Dark Maze*, by Thomas Adcock
1990   *The Man Who Would Be F. Scott Fitzgerald* ,
        by David Handler
1989   *The Rain*, by Keith Peterson
1988   *The Telling of Lies*, by Timothy Findley
1987   *Bimbos of the Death Sun*, by Sharyn McCrumb
1986   *The Junkyard Dog*, by Robert Campbell
1985   *Pigs Get Fat*, by Warren Murphy
1984   *Grandmaster*, by Warren Murphy and Molly Cochran
1983   *Mrs. White*, by Margaret Tracy
1982   *Triangle*, by Teri White
1981   *The Old Dick*, by L. A. Morse
1980   *Public Murders*, by Bill Granger
1979   *The Hog Murders*, by William L. DeAndrea
1978   *Deceit and Deadly Lies*, by Franklin Bandy
1977   *The Quark Maneuver*, by Mike Jahn
1976   *Confess, Fletch*, by Gregory McDonald
1975   *Autopsy*, by John R. Feegel
1974   *The Corpse That Walked*, by Roy Winsor
1973   *Death of an Informer*, by Will Perry
1972   *The Invader*, by Richard Wormser
1971   *For Murder I Charge More*, by Frank McAuliffe
1970   *Operation Flashpoint*, by Dan J. Marlowe

GRAND MASTER AWARDS
1993   Lawrence Block
1992   Donald E. Westlake
1991   Elmore Leonard
1990   Tony Hillerman
1989   Helen McCloy
1988   Hillary Waugh
1987   Phyllis A. Whitney
1986   Michael Gilbert
1985   Ed McBain (Evan Hunter)
1984   Dorothy Salisbury Davis

1983	John le Carré
1982	Margaret Millar
1981	Julian Symons
1980	Stanley Ellin
1979	W. R. Burnett
1978	Aaron Marc Stein
1977	Daphne du Maurier
	Dorothy B. Hughes
	Ngaio Marsh
1976	Graham Greene
1975	Eric Ambler
1974	(No Award)
1973	Ross Macdonald
1972	Judson Philips
1971	John D. MacDonald
1970	Mignon G. Eberhart
1969	James M. Cain
1968	John Creasey
1967	(No Award)
1966	Baynard Kendrick
1965	Georges Simenon
1964	(No Award)
1963	George Harmon Coxe
1962	John Dickson Carr
1961	Erle Stanley Gardner
1960	Ellery Queen
1959	(No Award)
1958	Rex Stout
1957	Vincent Starrett
1954	Agatha Christie

Bibliography

Barzun, Jacques, and Wendell Hertig Taylor. *A Catalogue of Crime*.
New York: Harper & Row, 1989.

Hardwick, Michael. *The Complete Guide to Sherlock Holmes*. New
York: St. Martin's Press, 1986.

Haycraft, Howard. *Murder for Pleasure*. New York: D. Appleton-
Century Co., 1941.

Horning, Jane. *The Mystery Lovers' Book of Quotations*. New York:
The Mysterious Press, 1988.

Hubin, Allen J. *Crime Fiction, 1749–1980: A Comprehensive Bibliography*. New York. Garland Publishing, Inc., 1984.

Hubin, Allen J. *1981–1985 Supplement to Crime Fiction, 1749–1984*.
New York: Garland Publishing, Inc., 1988.

Keating, H. R. F. *The Bedside Companion to Crime*. New York: The
Mysterious Press, 1989.

Malloy, William. *The Mystery Book of Days*. New York: The Mysterious Press, 1990.

Menendez, Albert. *The Subject Is Murder*. New York: Garland Publishing, Inc., 1986.

Ocork, Shannon. *How to Write Mysteries*. Cincinnati: Writer's Di-
gest, 1989.

Pronzini, Bill. *Gun in Cheek*. New York: The Mysterious Press, 1982.

Reilly, John M. (First and Second Editions); and Leslie Henderson (Third Edition), editors. *Twentieth Century Crime and Mystery Writers*. First and Second editions, New York: St. Martin's Press, 1980, 1985. Third edition, Chicago: St. James Press, 1991.

Steinbrunner, Chris, et al. *Detectionary*. Lock Haven, PA: Hammermill Paper Company, 1972.

Steinbrunner, Chris, and Penzler, Otto. *Encyclopedia of Mystery and Detection*. New York: McGraw-Hill, 1976.

Symons, Julian. *Bloody Murder,* Third Edition. New York: The Mysterious Press, 1992.

Winn, Dilys, editor. *Murder Ink: The Mystery Reader's Companion*. New York: Workman Publishing, 1977.

Winn, Dilys, editor. *Murderess Ink: The Better Half of the Mystery*. New York: Workman Publishing, 1979.

Index

Chandler, Raymond (*cont.*)
  on mystery writing, 92, 93, 96,
    138
  noted quotes from, 86, 69, 76,
    138
  uncompleted manuscript of, 95
Charles, Nick, 32–33, 135
Charles, Nora, 32, 33, 135
Charm School, The (Demille), 108,
  110
Charteris, Leslie, 21, 58, 129
Chase, James Hadley, 39, 142
Chee, Jim, 81
Chesbro, George C., 116–17
Chesterton, G. K., 29–30, 56
child detectives, 86
Children of Men, The (James), 97
Christie, Agatha, 11, 21, 34–37,
    61, 137
  archaeological themes of, 121
  background of, 34, 121
  Chandler on, 92
  Christmas mystery by, 122
  cozy mysteries by, 26, 50
  disappearance of, 95–96
  Edgar awarded to, 155
  exotic settings used by, 120,
    121, 127
  favorite U.S. mystery writer of,
    48
  films based on books of, 37, 144
  Miss Marple books by, 26, 29,
    36, 120
  Poirot character of, 29, 32,
    35–37, 70
  U.S. vs. British titles of, 73, 130
Christmas mysteries, 122–23
Christopher, Paul, 110–11, 125
Circular Staircase, The (Rinehart),
  26, 75
Clair, René, 144
Clark, Douglas, 60

Clay, Colonel, 16
Cleary, Jon, 152
Cleek, Hamilton, 54–55
Clemens, Samuel (Mark Twain),
  99, 118
Clemm, Virginia, 98
Clifford, Francis, 139
Clinton, Bill, 112
Clinton-Baddeley, V. C., 60
Cobb, Matt, 76, 135
Cochran, Molly, 154
Cohen, Anthea, 140
Cohen, Octavus Roy, 43
Coleridge, Samuel Taylor, 99
Coles, Manning, 74
Collins, Michael, 115, 153
Collins, Wilkie, 15, 56
Colorado, Kat, 82, 98
Conant, Susan, 138
Connelly, Michael, 152
Constantine, K. C., 65
Continental Op, 39–40, 42–43, 87
Cool, Bertha, 43, 133
Coombs, Murdo (Frederick C.
  Davis), 103
Cornwell, David John Moore
  (John le Carré), 105, 109,
    110, 111, 128, 152, 155
Cornwell, Patricia D., 52, 152
Correspondence-School Detec-
  tive, 23
Corris, Peter, 126
Cortez, Ricardo, 40
Coxe, George Harmon, 155
Coyne, Brady, 84
cozy mysteries, 26, 50, 131
Craig, Jonathan, 44
Crais, Robert, 137
Creasey, John, 57, 65, 93, 143,
  155
  twenty-four pseudonyms of,
    101